A SCOTSMAN'S
KISS

A SCOTSMAN'S KISS

•

Frances Engle Wilson

AVALON BOOKS
THOMAS BOUREGY AND COMPANY, INC.
401 LAFAYETTE STREET
NEW YORK, NEW YORK 10003

PRINTED IN THE UNITED STATES OF AMERICA
ON ACID-FREE PAPER
BY HADDON CRAFTSMEN, BLOOMSBURG, PENNSYLVANIA

To the memory of Max, our beautiful
black cocker, who stayed beside my
desk as I wrote, added joy to our lives,
and gave us his unending devotion.

If a lady of strong will like you,
Should meet a Scotsman with purpose true,
Take care lassie and remember this,
You'll ne'er escape from a Scotsman's kiss.

—F. E. W.

make an arrangement with you for the use of Hampton House.''

Abby's face was a picture of astonishment. ''Use my house! You can't be serious.''

''Oh believe me, I'm totally serious. This fine old house of yours can provide exactly the interior sets the script of *A Different Drummer* calls for. Why, the Federal Period architecture of Hampton House is perfect in every detail, inside as well as out. That along with the authentic antique furnishings make it ideal for this film.''

''How can you know that? You haven't even seen anything of this house but the front hall and this back parlor.'' She flung out her hand in a gesture of impatience.

''Oh that's not exactly true,'' he said calmly, giving her a benign smile. ''You see, I did a bit of research before I came here. In going through copies of *Colonial Homes* magazine I found articles on numerous historic homes of New England. One issue featured Federal Period homes in New Hampshire and Hampton House was shown, with color photographs of the formal parlor, the dining room, and one bedroom. There were detailed descriptions of the wall coverings, wood moldings, and the carvings on cornices and chair rails. So you see I do know that Hampton House is the authentic setting Allied Studios wants for this major production.''

''That's some sales pitch you hand out, Rome

Douglas, and I'm sorry to rain on your parade," Abby said, an apologetic note in her voice, "but I live here, and I have my antique shop here, as you know. It would completely disrupt my life if I were to allow you to do this. I'm sure you can understand that's why it's out of the question." She softened her words by following them with a regretful smile. "I hate to disappoint you on this, but I'm sure you can find another house that's suitable."

Rome frowned, his eyes studying her with a curious intensity. "Hold on, Abby. You're jumping to the wrong conclusions about this. Believe me, I have no intention of disrupting your normal living schedule. In fact, I promise my total cooperation to insure that you are not inconvenienced by this."

She looked skeptical. "You hold on, Rome. A film crew at work in my house can hardly be considered anything but inconvenient. My antique business would be kaput for the duration for one thing, and—"

"Now wait a minute," Rome interrupted her, holding up a silencing hand. "Just hear me out. All Allied Studios asks is to use the downstairs rooms in Hampton House for film sets. In fact, I'll stipulate this in the agreement and specify that it includes only the main parlor, the dining room, the entrance hall, and possibly the staircase and the upper landing for one of those grand scenes that all period movies consider a must. The shot where the glamorous leading lady slowly descends the stairs wearing a magnificent ball gown, trailing a bejeweled hand along the balustrade. You couldn't deny them that, now could you?'' he said in a cajoling voice as he offered her his special charm-laden smile. ''And to make it all worthwhile, you'll be paid quite a considerable sum for every day of filming here. You can add a lot of antiques to your inventory with the money Allied is willing to pay you, Abby, in case that would interest you.''

She hadn't stopped to consider that she could make a lot of money out of this setup. It was an appealing thought, and certainly she could take a little inconvenience for a few weeks if the price was right. She sat forward in her chair, inclining her head toward Rome. ''Of course that interests me,'' she said. ''Anything I can do to enhance my antique business is important to me.''

''Well then, you'll be glad to know that when the credits roll, not only will it state that *A Different Drummer* was filmed on location here, but also that the interior furnishings were by Hampton House Antiques,'' he said with quiet emphasis.

''It'll really say that?''

''Absolutely.'' He confirmed it with a decisive nod. ''That will be a nice bit of advertising for your business. Don't you think?''

''It certainly would be.'' She contemplated the possibility, a pleased expression on her face. ''You know, you're good at this job of yours.''

"Thanks." He nodded perfunctorily. "I do try to give it my best shot."

"Yes, I'd say you do. You're very persuasive too." She smiled and leaned back in her chair, crossing her arms across her chest. "I never thought I could be talked into something like this in a million years, much less in only one hour. Also, I'm still not sure I won't live to regret it. But be that as it may, you've convinced me that I have more to gain than I have to lose." Abby shrugged. "You've won me over," she said, with a sigh and a tight little laugh.

"That's great!" Rome's voice had a jubilant ring. He immediately extended his hand, taking Abby's in a firm handshake. "I'll get right with this, talk with Allied, settle all the details we've talked about, and get back to you late this afternoon with a contract, if that's okay."

She nodded. "Sure, that's fine." Rome still held her hand, so Abby eased it from his warm grasp and stood up.

Rome rose quickly too, and together they walked from the room. "You're going to be glad you're doing this," he assured her. "It's bound to prove interesting and fun. Why, you'll be the envy of everyone in Lindenwood because you'll have close contact with some big-name superstars. That should make things exciting, don't you think so?"

"I suppose," she said, making a slight grimace. "But I'm really not much of a movie buff, and I'm not turned on by celebrities unless they've truly done something to merit people's respect and admiration.''

Her reaction seemed to surprise Rome. ''I can go along with that. Fortunately, though, I think you'll approve of the two big-name stars they've signed for leading roles in *A Different Drummer*. They're real talents and pretty much deserve their celebrity status, Lee Greenway and Stephanie Marlowe.''

Abby brightened hearing this. ''You're right. Those two are great choices. I have to admit I'm impressed.''

''Then there's an up-and-coming newcomer, Drew Daniels.''

Startled, Abby drew in her breath in an audible gasp. Reeling as if she'd been struck, Abby quickly reached out and grabbed hold of the front door handle to steady herself.

Apparently Rome took no notice of her disturbed reaction. He went right on with what he was saying. ''You may not have heard of this Daniels fellow because he's just recently begun getting the meaty parts. He's young, handsome, and considered *strictly cool* I'm told. At least, I know they were plenty eager to get him for the part of the younger brother to Greenway's character.''

Abby lowered her head to hide her tortured expression. ''I've heard of him,'' she said, and there was little if any inflection in her voice. Without further comment she opened the front door and stepped aside for Rome to leave.

Chapter Two

Abby closed the front door without actually being aware of what she was doing. The impact of Rome's announcement about Drew had her mind in turmoil. The last thing in this world she wanted was to have to look at Drew's arrogant, smiling face again, or to have to listen to another of his cunning lies. And no way under heaven did she want him to spend even five minutes inside Hampton House.

A minute later, still quaking like an aspen leaf, she yanked open the door and dashed outside. "Wait," she screamed. "Come back—I've changed my mind." Frantically waving her hands in the air, Abby raced toward the driveway.

Rome had his head turned, looking over his shoulder as he backed his car rapidly down the tree-lined drive. Obviously he didn't see her, and apparently he couldn't hear her over the sound of his car's engine. Abby watched in despair as Rome reached the end of the drive, swung his car around, and wheeled off down the street.

Energized by her panic, Abby ran back in the house, grabbing up her car keys and purse. Her only thought now was to go after Rome. Get to him before he had time to contact his studio. Put a halt to this before it went a bit further.

In a New England village the size of Lindenwood, that fancy sports car of his would be easy to spot. There was no doubt in her mind that Rome Douglas was staying at the Lindenwood Inn. For of all the widely advertised New England inns, the elegant, turn-of-the-century Lindenwood was truly outstanding and afforded a breathtaking view of the White Mountains. A man who sought out scenic locations and interesting settings would only choose to stay there.

These thoughts flashed through her mind as she rushed through the kitchen, out the back door, and along the covered walkway that led from the main house to the adjoining old carriage house. This white clapboard structure still maintained its original eighteenth-century charm. And since less than one-third of it was used as a garage, she hoped before too long to convert the sizable remaining area into a shop for her antiques.

Having convinced herself that she was going to be able to locate Rome with little or no difficulty, Abby took a slow, calming breath, and slid in under the steering wheel of her worn but worthy Chevrolet Blazer. She placed the key in the ignition, then paused, taking her hand away without starting the motor. Her eyes narrowed now in a perplexed frown.

Wait a minute here! Don't go off half-cocked and

do something really stupid, she cautioned herself. She raised her head, thrusting her chin out at a stubborn angle, determined to put a rein on her emotions and let reason and common sense take over.

Why, she'd be a fool to blow this deal with Allied Studios simply because Drew was playing a part in the film. What was wrong with her memory? Didn't she remember all that Drew had cost her four years ago? Was she now going to be dumb enough to let him cost her even more? No, she was not! "No way," she spit out the words, accompanying them by pounding the steering wheel twice with her fist.

A second later a defiant little smile moved across Abby's lips as she removed the car key from the ignition and climbed out of the Blazer. She didn't leave the garage. She simply stood there quietly, still smiling as she gazed around at the large, unused area. She knew that the money she was going to get for allowing *A Different Drummer* to be filmed in Hampton House would pay for remodeling this carriage house, converting it into the antique shop she'd dreamed of having someday. She'd come to her senses just in the nick of time, because thanks to Rome Douglas and Allied Studios, that someday was now.

The whole idea of it gave her a delicious feeling. She spun around and marched out of the garage. As she hightailed it back to the house, she was humming a line from an old Broadway show tune—"everything's coming up roses . . .'' She'd not let Drew Daniels disrupt her life again. He'd called her a quaint, shy little New England pigeon that summer four years ago. But she was older and much wiser now. That once easily duped pigeon had now learned to spread her wings and soar like an eagle—hadn't she? Well, at least she was giving it her best try.

At this time in June the summer tourist season was getting underway all through the White Mountains. This very week both the New England National Brass and Gas Antique Car Tour and the Old-Time Fiddlers' Contest were taking place near Lindenwood at Loon Mountain. These events brought lots of visitors to the area, and fortunately for Abby many of these visitors were also antique shoppers.

Shortly after lunch a couple of customers came in, and throughout the afternoon there was a small but steady stream of people coming in to browse and leisurely examine the antiques Abby had on display.

One collector was quick to purchase some of the better pieces of Sandwich glass, as well as a Bennington hound-handled pitcher. Later a man with a western drawl that sounded as if he'd stepped out of a John Wayne movie, bought two large copper kettles for himself, and a set of six Haviland demitasse cups and saucers that he said he was taking home to ''my little woman.'' One middle-aged couple spent the better part of an hour considering a Chippendale fire screen with a petit-point scene. They finally left without it, but came back just before five o'clock and bought it.

Well pleased with the sales for the day, Abby was preparing to close up when the door chimes sang out again. It was rather late for another customer she thought, but with a shrug she opened the door to find a tall, broad-shouldered man wearing tan Dockers, an open-collar yellow knit golf shirt, and a leather camera case slung over his shoulder. He had a weathered face, large dark eyes, and a smattering of gray streaks in his hair that only made him appear more interesting. Abby had time for all these observations before he took a step closer to the door, smiled pleasantly, then spoke to her in a low-keyed voice. "I was supposed to meet the Scotsman here, but I don't see his car. I expect I beat him here, didn't I." The way he said it, it was half a question and half a statement of fact.

Totally puzzled, Abby stared at him, shaking her head slowly. "Who's the Scotsman? I'm afraid I don't know what you're talking about?"

"The Scotsman—that's Rome Douglas," he explained. "Everybody he works with calls him that. You will too when you get to know him." He smiled warmly and added, "Rome was on the phone with the studio when I left him, but I'm sure he'll be along in a few minutes. I'll just come in and get started, if it's okay with you."

Abby hesitated a second. "I guess that's all right,"

she said, opening the door rather reluctantly. "Exactly what are you to get started doing?"

The fellow chuckled wryly. "I guess the Scotsman didn't tell you about me—right?"

"Right, he didn't," she agreed, frowning.

"Sorry about that." He extended his hand to her. "I'm Brent Ritchey," he said, giving her hand a firm shake. "I'm to take pictures of the rooms in your house. Preliminary shots of furnishings and stuff Rome will need to work up the set designs."

"Oh. I—I see. I guess I see." Unconsciously her brow furrowed. Abby found it disconcerting, if not a bit irritating, that Rome had sent someone to take pictures of the rooms of her house without notifying her ahead of time. He certainly hadn't wasted any time getting about his business once she'd agreed to let him use her house. Who was this . . . this "Scotsman"? She smiled inwardly as she contemplated the possibility that Rome Douglas actually was of Scottish heritage. This was something she would have to find out about.

It was more than half an hour later when Rome arrived. "Man, I really apologize for not getting here sooner. I got hung up on the phone and then had to wait for the studio to fax me with the final contract details," Rome explained in a rush of words. "Sure hope Brent's picture-taking hasn't been a bother."

At this, a suggestion of annoyance hovered in Abby's eyes, but she managed a thin smile and a shrug. "I could have used a little warning is all. I almost didn't let him in. He kept talking about the Scotsman, and I didn't have a clue as to who that might be.'' She chided him in her casual, jesting way.

Rome grinned sheepishly. ''I'm sorry about that. Guess I need to clarify a few things for you, don't I?''

''Yeah, that would be helpful.''

''Well, I'll do that tonight when I take you out to dinner.''

''I hadn't heard that you and I were having dinner together tonight.'' Abby's mouth twitched with amusement. ''Is every Scotsman as sure of himself and as direct as you are?''

Laughter flickered in his eyes as they met hers. ''I don't know about all the Scots, but we of the Douglas clan find that a positive approach gets the best results. Besides, you and I have a few business details to iron out. So why not do that over dinner?''

''Why not,'' she replied with a gracious smile. ''Who am I to differ with the clan of Douglas?''

Rome's laugh was deep, warm, and rich. ''Okay then. Give me about twenty minutes to check on Brent and make sure he's taken all the pictures I want. After that, we'll head out for dinner. I hear there's a good restaurant in a converted Colonial house that's fairly close by.''

''You're talking about the Foxglove Tavern. It's an interesting place. You'll like the setting. Might even want it in your film.''

''Yeah. I figured I ought to check it out.'' He gave

her a little shove toward the stairs as he walked across the entry hall, toward the front parlor. ''Get yourself ready. I'll work with Brent and then be waiting for you here by the stairs. Don't be long,'' he cautioned.

The Scotsman sure was bossy, and adept at getting others to go along with him, she thought as she scurried up the stairs. Although she did admit that he had managed to manipulate her rather charmingly, at that.

As quickly as she could, she changed out of her jeans and button-down–collared shirt that was her usual workday attire and put on a butter-yellow skirt and a matching yellow blouse that had white piping around the collar and sleeves. It took her an additional seven minutes to freshen her makeup, add a slight touch of violet eye shadow, and comb her jet-black hair so it curled softly around her face, allowing a few wispy bangs to fall across her forehead.

Rome was waiting at the bottom of the stairs, casually leaning against the newel post, gazing up at her as she descended. ''Hey there, aren't you a pretty yellow bird. Right on time, too.''

Abby came to an abrupt stop midway down the stairs, for Rome's greeting spun wheels in her memory. She remembered when another man had called her a pigeon—a dull, gray, uninteresting bird, the pigeon. This label and all that had happened that particular summer had made her think of herself as a woman without savvy—without appeal. Now a man, an attractive man, was calling her a pretty yellow bird. She liked that. A yellow bird is colorful, charming, even arresting. This was a lovely idea to contemplate. She wished she could keep hold of it, but she couldn't, for such feelings are fleeting and as fragile as soap bubbles. . . .

It was only a short drive from Hampton House to the Foxglove Tavern. Customer parking was at the rear, and Abby and Rome ambled slowly around to the front entrance. The June evening breeze carried the fragrance of lilac blossoms, viburnum, and the scarlet climbing roses that spilled over the fence that bordered the property.

It was dusk, but there was still enough light to see the details of this old Colonial cottage. Its weathered shingles abutting cornerboards recalled the simple architecture of a simpler age. And once inside, the gun-stock posts and ceiling beams illustrated the exposed framing that gave the rooms of Early Colonial homes their warmth and character.

Rome asked if they might have one of the small tables at the far side of the huge brick fireplace that was the focal point of the dining room at the Foxglove. The tavern keeper, a big lumberjack of a man with a florid face, nodded agreeably and immediately led them to the chosen table, and handed them menus.

"Abby, you've eaten here before. Tell me, what's the house specialty?" Rome asked, not bothering to open the menu.

"That depends. Are you a big meat and potato guy?"

"I'm plenty hungry, if that's what you mean. I had lunch on the run, and that was only a ham sandwich and coffee."

"Then I heartily recommend the London broil. It's great."

He glanced across the table at her. "Sounds fine to me. Is that what you're having?"

"Oh no," She shook her head emphatically. "That's more food than I can handle. They have a chicken with tarragon that is simply delicious, and exactly right for me."

"Well then, I'd say that about settles what we're each going to eat." There was humor in his eyes and a pleasant curve to his mouth as he continued to look at her in a way that made it obvious that he was finding her both pleasing to look at and entertaining to be with.

A second later a waiter appeared to fill their water glasses and take their dinner order. As soon as he left, Abby turned her full attention to Rome. "Back at the house you said you had some business to take up with me. I expect that means you have a contract for me to sign."

His expressive face became serious. "It's in my briefcase in the car. We'll get to it after we eat, but first I want to tell you several things I found out today when I talked to the studio." He leaned forward, placing one hand on the table. "I found out about the shooting schedule. It's all set. They plan to start film-ing here in Lindenwood the second week in July.''

"That soon! Why, that's less than three weeks away.'' Abby's voice spiraled in surprise.

"Do you have a problem with that?'' he asked, a look of discomfort crossing his face.

"No, no,'' she assured him quickly. "Of course I don't. It just surprised me that it would come about that quickly.'' She looked at him with amused wonder. "You work faster than any man I've ever seen. Time is money—and every second counts. Right?''

"That's about it, Abby.'' A flash of humor flickered in his eyes as they met hers. "And speaking of money, you'll be happy to know that you'll be getting paid more for the use of your house than I originally told you.''

"Why is that?''

"Well, first off, we were figuring on four to six weeks for the location shoot, and filming the rest on the lot in California. But your mayor was so cooper-ative, and Lindenwood offers more than we antici-pated. More than that, Hampton House, with your antique furnishings, surpasses our greatest expecta-tions. All of it makes it reasonable to shoot the entire film right here. That means eight to ten weeks—more days—more dough. Simple case of mathematics.'' He flashed her a grin. "I take it you have no objection to getting more money.''

"None whatsoever,'' she said, breaking into a wide,

open smile. "I have a wonderful use for the money, I assure you."

"Great. I was a little worried that you might balk at the extended time. Especially since you're not high on movie people in the first place," he said candidly.

"Oh forget that." She waved her hand in a negative gesture. "Bad first reaction. That's all." She passed it off with a shrug. "I've had all day to think about this whole thing, and I've mellowed. I'm truly enthusiastic about it now, no fooling."

"Whew." Rome whistled a sigh of relief, his eyes scrutinizing her closely. "You'll never know how glad I am to hear you say that." He paused and rubbed his forefinger back and forth across his chin, continuing to study her face. "Because there's one more little thing I need to tell you."

She narrowed her eyes in a sudden frown. "I'm leery of the way you said *little thing*. Makes me think I'm not going to like it somehow."

"What if I say minor thing? Would that sound better to you."

"Not much."

At that moment their waiter reappeared to serve their dinner. He hovered around, passing a straw basket of dinner rolls, pouring a cup of coffee for Rome, and bringing lemon wedges for Abby's iced tea. She took a sip of her tea and waited for him to finish waiting on them before saying anything more to Rome.

"Everything looks delicious, doesn't it," she said,

as she unfolded her napkin and laid it across her lap. "What say we eat now and you can lay that minor little whatever on me after we've enjoyed our dinner."

"I'll vote for that," he agreed.

They were both hungry and they attacked the meal with gusto, their conversation limited to a few comments on how good the food tasted. Midway through, Rome leaned forward to take another roll from the bread basket and at the same time spoke to Abby in a quiet voice. "Don't look right now, but there are two men at a table near the middle of the room. One has his back to you, but the other fellow has been watching you ever since they came in. In fact, the way he's been scrutinizing both of us, I think he's a jealous lover trying to figure out who the stranger is who's out with his girl."

"I think you see too many movies," Abby whispered back to him. At the same time she shifted slightly in her chair, slid her napkin off her lap, then bent over to retrieve it and at the same time look over at the table Rome had described. When she sat back up in her chair, she gave Rome an arch look. "You've got a wild imagination, you know that?" She made a wry face at him and laughed. "Those are two good citizens of Lindenwood. The older man with his back to us is Nicholas Hurd, a loan officer at the bank. The one you claim has been eyeing me is Joe Wheeler, a thoroughly nice guy that I went to high school with who now has the General Motors agency here. I'd say they were having a business dinner together just like we are. I'm sure the word is out about your filming a movie here. They're not looking at me, they're just interested in checking out *the Scotsman*.''

''Well, if you say so. But I still think that young guy is more concerned with you than with me.''

''If so, it's only because his wife will insist on hearing a detailed report on our being together, and how we appear to react to each other.'' She shrugged. ''She's a good friend of mine, and I really do like her. Kay is one of those friends, however, who likes nothing better than playing matchmaker for her unmarried chums. She's been trying to pair me off with every new man that comes on the scene for ages. I pity ol' Joe, 'cause when he gets home tonight Kay will swab him down for every tiny last detail about you. Tomorrow you'll be fodder for her marriage mill. So don't say I didn't warn you,'' she added. Abby's tone was sympathetic, but there was a teasing glint in her eyes. '' 'Course, you could fend her off by letting it be known that you have a bonny Scottish lassie awaiting you on the banks of Loch Lomond.''

''I couldn't rightly say that, seeing that I've not been to Scotland. Although I'm planning on getting there one of these days, before too long.'' A mischievous look flashed in his eyes. ''I was planning to find a pretty lassie to take with me when I go.''

''California doesn't lack for beautiful women. You'll find one.''

"I intend to," he said with conviction. "And not necessarily in California."

She regarded him with a speculative gaze. The light, bantering tone that had been going on between them had suddenly changed somehow, and she didn't quite understand why. Wanting to steer their conversation into a different vein, she said, "I think I'm ready now to hear whatever it was you needed to tell me about the film schedule for *A Different Drummer.*" She tried to appear relaxed and casual as she picked up her fork and resumed her dinner.

"Oh there's no hurry. You're still eating your chicken. We can take up that remaining bit of business after dinner."

Abby detected an uneasy note in his voice. She eyed him frowning. "I thought the whole purpose of our having dinner was to settle our business. So let me hear the rest of it." There was more than a hint of exasperation in her voice now, for she sensed that he was going to lay something on her that she wasn't going to like very much.

"All right then, let me explain some aspects of your contract to you," he said, the lines of concentration deepening along his brows and under his eyes. "You'll see when you read it that the studio has agreed to pay you double the figure I quoted you this morning. You can accomplish plenty with that amount of money," he added, with a significant lifting of his brows.

"Yes, and I intend to," she said, tilting her chin up at a confident angle.

"There were several reasons why Allied raised the daily fee for filming in your house."

"I know. You told me it was because they now intend to shoot the entire movie here. Right?"

Rome nodded. "That and the fact that they will film more of it at Hampton House."

Abby eyed him with a critical squint. "The more days they use my house, the more money I make. You've already said that. So why are you saying it again?"

"Because it involves a little more than that."

"What more?" The tensing of her jaw betrayed her frustration. "Get to the point!"

The line of Rome's mouth tightened a fraction. "I'm sure you can understand that with added footage being shot they will require more extensive use of areas in your house."

"I suppose so," she said matter-of-factly, giving him a bland smile. "And for that kind of money they can turn their cameras on the kitchen, the back parlor, and all over the entire downstairs." She paused to lay her knife and fork across her now empty plate and to brush her napkin across her lips, then added, "They can even have the staircase for that fancy dress ball scene you said was a requirement in a grand epic movie like *A Different Drummer*." She mocked him in a playful manner.

Rome was not amused. His expression was more one of pained tolerance. "That's all well and good Abby, but it's going to be necessary now to also use that bedroom that was pictured in the magazine I told you I researched, and the nursery and child's play-room, all of which are in the upstairs west wing of the house."

"I'm aware of where those rooms are located, Rome," she said coolly, her expression taut and de-risive. "And I made it quite clear right from the start that the upstairs of Hampton House is off limits for your movie. We had a rather lengthy discussion about this before I agreed to have any part in this whole project. Have you suddenly forgotten that?"

The line of Rome's mouth tightened another frac-tion. "No. I have not," he answered tersely.

"Well then, why didn't you make my wishes clear to your studio?" she countered icily.

"I did, Abby. I explained the conditions under which you would agree to let us film in Hampton House. In fact, that's why it took me all afternoon to negotiate your contract."

"It doesn't sound like I came out too well at that." She glared at him with reproachful eyes.

"Just listen to me a minute. Let me tell you some good points." He smiled benignly, as if dealing with a temperamental child. "You can rest assured that your own bedroom wing area will be roped off. No actors or actresses, no cameramen, nobody at all will come near your area. Even a portion of the upstairs landing on your side will be secured. Your privacy will not be invaded, believe me.'' He paused, as if he expected her to comment on this. Abby looked at him, moved her head in a barely discernible nod, but didn't say anything. ''Also,'' he continued. ''To minimize any inconvenience for you, what filming is done upstairs will be completed in one trip. What I mean is the camera equipment and all will be moved upstairs, all the scenes completed, and then everything removed. They will come upstairs only for these few brief shoots.''

''How few and how brief are we talking about here?'' she asked glumly.

''Well, I haven't seen the final script, so I don't know exactly how many scenes, but I doubt that it will take more than three or four days, a week tops.''

Abby had a closed expression, her eyes hooded, her full mouth tucked at the corners. ''I'm not happy about this. It really upsets me.''

''I know,'' he said gently. ''I'm sorry.'' His tone was apologetic. ''Would it help if I told you that I'd be there each of those days to make sure you're caused the least inconvenience possible?''

Abby's expression had grown even more clenched. Then with what seemed like a great effort of will on her part, it became flat again, like a piece of paper that had been smoothed out. ''Yes,'' she said softly. ''That might help.''

Chapter Three

Rome and Abby left the Foxglove shortly after nine. When they got back to Hampton House, Rome handed her the Allied contract, saying, "We can discuss this further after you've had time to check it over. I'll call you and come pick it up sometime tomorrow, if that's okay with you."

"Anytime," she said, nodding affirmatively. "I'll have it signed and ready."

With a quick "good night," he left her. And as soon as Abby heard his car drive off, she locked the front door, then began walking slowly around the downstairs arranging the lights and getting everything set for the night. This was a routine habit and she did it without conscious thought, because her mind was still dwelling on the events of the past few hours.

She was very much aware that she had overreacted to almost everything that Rome and she had talked about. She also knew the reason why. It was this that made her angry. Not with Rome, of course, but with herself. After all, the movie studio was paying her a phenomenal sum in order to film inside her house. Certainly that gave them the right to use every room

they wanted to—downstairs, upstairs, the whole
works. She couldn't object. She wouldn't object if it
weren't for Drew. She slapped the wall switch at the
bottom of the stairs, turning on the chandelier on the
upper landing, angry tensions building inside her. She
didn't mind the camera crew and all the other actors
going everywhere. It was only Drew. None of it would
bother her if only he was not part of it. Abby's eyes
darkened like fierce thunderclouds. She hated the
thought of Drew walking through the rooms of her
wonderful old house. She despised the idea of him
eyeing her antiques, calculating their value, his schem-
ing mind figuring out a way to con her a second time.

She clenched her hands into fists and stormed up
the stairs. Well, she'd not sacrifice a family treasure
for the likes of him ever again. No way! Anger rose
to her face, drawing her mouth taut. The thought of
that porcelain table clock with the figure of an Italian
shepherd sent a stab of pain to her heart. From her
childhood she had loved the porcelain figure of the
shepherd boy that sat atop that clock with his green
pointed hat, his brown fitted trousers, and his long tu-
nic shirt that was patterned in rose, green, and yellow.
She was fascinated by the shepherd's crook he held in
his hand, and she adored the soulful-eyed, black and
white dog that sat at the boy's feet.

The image of the boy and his dog stayed on her
mind as she marched purposefully into her bedroom,
turned on the bedside lamp, placed the book she was

reading on the nightstand, and folded back the coverlet on her four-poster bed.

She undressed and got ready for bed, all the time berating herself for allowing the practiced charm of a phony like Drew to make a dupe of her. In the bathroom a clownish reflection, woeful and ludicrous at once, confronted her now in the mirror, eyes fogged with tears, mouth foaming with toothpaste. "Boy, you're one pathetic pigeon, Abby Hampton," she said aloud, eyeing her image in the mirror. Then she filled her mouth with mint-flavored gargle, swished it around her teeth, and spit it out with a vengeance. Tossing her head and lifting her chin up at a defiant angle, she looked at her reflection one more time. "Now," she said with a cocky smile. "That's more like a yellow bird."

It was mid-afternoon the following day before Rome telephoned her. "Hi, Abby," he greeted her with a cheery voice. "Are you busy? Got a customer?" he asked.

"Nope, not now. Had a few earlier today, but it's been slow going since lunch."

"I was hoping you were free. I've got something to show you. Could you take off for a while and come meet me?"

"I—I guess so. When?"

"Could you make it right away?" He sounded eager and a bit mysterious. All of which made Abby curious.

"Sure, where are you?"

"I'm near the square. I'll meet you in front of the courthouse. Can you make it in fifteen minutes?"

"Yeah, but what's this all about anyway?"

"I'll tell you when you get here," he said, signing off quickly without giving her an opportunity to question him further.

If Rome wanted to arouse her interest, he'd certainly managed to do it. Abby was totally intrigued by his words and manner. So she wasted no time in hanging out the closed sign and driving down to the center of Lindenwood, which was four blocks squared around a courtyard, with the gray-stone courthouse standing on the north side, like a small castle blocking the rest of the town from the worst winter winds. In the middle of the town square was a brass statue dedicated to the valiant men of New Hampshire who had lost their lives in the early wars. Small boys climbed on the statue to sit on the cannons. And there was also a fountain which children played in in the summer, and flower gardens, sidewalks, and a few trees—including especially one towering evergreen which was always decorated for Christmas.

Abby caught sight of Rome as she approached the square. He was standing by the only empty parking space close to the courthouse. She wondered if he'd had to strong-arm anybody in order to save it for her.

As she climbed out of the Blazer, he grabbed hold of her arm and steered her rapidly down the sidewalk. "Where are we going?" she asked breathlessly.

"Down this block, then over there and around the corner." He pointed across the street and waved his hand to indicate a farther distance.

"Unless there's a deadline we have to meet, could we slow down?" She was all but galloping to keep pace with Rome's long stride.

Rome immediately shortened his step and slowed down to an easy walk. "I'm sorry," he said, his face creasing into that easy smile of his. "I guess I'm too eager to get your reaction to what I've found for you."

She eyed him questioningly. "Found for me? What on earth are you talking about?"

"You'll see in a few minutes," he said, looping his arm through hers.

"But I want to know about it now," she demanded stubbornly. "So tell me."

"No can do, Abby. That would spoil the surprise." He quirked an eyebrow at her and smiled. They had reached the end of the block. Rome's hand glided under her elbow, taking hold of her arm with practiced ease. He steered her across the street, around the corner, and halfway down the side street before he stopped and pulled a key out of his pants pocket.

Abby's eyes held a baffled expression. "This is a vacant store."

"Yeah, I know," he said, sounding complacent. "It

happens to be the only available space anywhere near the center of town."

"That's important?" Her voice echoed her bewilderment.

"It is if you want to sell to the busloads of tourists that I understand flock through here on those fall foliage tours. A shop in a central location close to the town square would be ideal. Don't you agree?" He had the door unlocked now and he stepped back so she could enter. "Go in and look around," he urged. "It's nice and clean. The owner told me they'd just finished giving the walls a fresh coat of paint. Nice color too. He called it antique ivory. I'd say that's most appropriate for a place that features antiques."

Abby was walking around looking the place over as Rome was talking. She spun around now and eyed him inquiringly. "Are you planning on turning this into a store that you'll use some way in your movie?" she asked.

"No. The studio and I are planning on you moving your antique shop down here so you can carry on your business while we're shooting the movie in your house. In fact, I've been authorized by Allied to lease this space for your shop, and to take care of all the arrangements to move your inventory and set everything up the way you want it."

Abby gaped at him in astonishment. "Why would they do all that?"

"Because it's a perfect solution for you and for us,"

he answered, his air of cool self-assurance arousing her skepticism.

"How's that? What's in it for them?" She gave him an arch glance.

Rome's expressive face remained serious and calm. "Well, in order to set up the rooms in Hampton House to be ready to start filming, all the various things that are part of your shop have to be cleared out and put away. Rather than pay to put them in storage, it was my suggestion that we provide a suitable location from which you can operate your antique business during the period we are using your home. It not only makes good sense, it's good business." He directed a long, keen scrutiny at Abby as he said this. Then he paused for a second, shrugged, and then added, "Seems to me it's a no-lose deal. Everybody's a winner."

Abby studied Rome with somber curiosity. Why had he gone to the trouble of arranging all of this, she wondered? It couldn't be just for her convenience. Maybe after last night he'd been afraid that she was going to back out on him—renege on her agreement to let him have her house. But he had no reason to think that. She'd promised to have the contract with Allied signed and ready for him today. He hadn't needed to bribe her by providing a location for a temporary shop. On the other hand, he did realize that she was upset about the expanded use of all the areas of her house. Rome did appear sensitive to her feelings in this. Probably he'd done all of this in an effort to pacify her so she'd accept his studio's conditions with good grace, she thought with a sigh.

"Yeah, you're right Rome. You movie guys sure do think of everything," she said, letting a smile erase her frown. "Everybody *is* a winner."

"Then I take it that this setup is okay with you." He made a sweeping gesture with his hand around the vacant shop.

"It's more than okay—it's great. And I might add, so are you." The enthusiasm in her voice matched her broadening smile.

"We Scotsmen aim to please," he said, a flash of good humor crossing his face. "Now, while you check out the storage room and stuff in the back area, I'll just go find a phone and let this Thornton Frost fellow know he's got himself a new tenant."

"Oh sure, Thorny Frost does own this building. I'd forgotten that. He's quite an interesting character around here as a matter of fact. He claims his grandfather was a distant cousin of Robert Frost, and Thorny is by way of being a poet too."

"I might have guessed that, because when I picked up the key from him he didn't strike me as your typical property-owning businessman. Those dark, penetrating eyes of his had a secret expression, and his face had the craggy look of unfinished sculpture."

"That's an amazing description of Thorny. You

really have a camera's eye for faces as well as for movie settings. You don't miss a single detail. I'm impressed.''

He passed her compliment off with a brief shrug. ''At times I overlook an item or two, but this Frost guy has a look about him that catches your attention. You see him once and you remember him.'' Rome took a step away from her, turning as if he were going to leave. Then he swung back around to face her. ''Say, tell me, is our landlord much of a poet?''

Abby crossed her arms and pursed her lips thoughtfully. ''He's no Robert Frost of course, but then, who is?'' She walked over to him. ''I will tell you this. Thornton's poems are well received around here, and if you'd like to hear him read some of his works I'll take you to the Festival of Poetry that's held late in July at the house where Robert Frost once lived, up at Franconia. Each summer a number of poets from around New Hampshire give readings in the old barn at the Frost place. Does a long summer evening of poetry reading grab you?'' she asked facetiously.

Rome grimaced. ''I'm afraid I'm really not into poetry, Abby.''

''I thought you might not be.'' She managed to suppress a smile.

''On the other hand,'' he countered quickly. ''I'm definitely and totally into spending evenings with you.'' He reached out and cupped her shoulders between his hands. ''And as long as you're sitting beside me I'm game for anything!'' He let his hands slide caressingly off her shoulders, then turned and left the shop to make his phone call.

Chapter Four

Abby rarely opened her antique shop before ten in the morning, so she was surprised to hear the the front doorbell being rung with repeated insistence when the tall clock in the entry hall indicated the time was only a quarter till nine. Her surprise vanished when she opened the door to find Kay Wheeler standing there, her curly mass of brown hair blown awry, her face pink with eagerness, and curiosity sparkling in her amber eyes.

"What took you so long?" Abby greeted her with barely suppressed laughter. "I'd begun to think that Joe forgot to report that he'd seen me having dinner with a strange man at the Foxglove Tavern night before last."

"Of course he told me all about it. He wouldn't dare not to." She grinned and came inside. "And I did come as quick as I could. I had a jillion errands to run yesterday morning, and then when I did call you in the afternoon, you didn't answer." She planted her hands on her hips, feigning annoyance. "I was frantic to hear about everything. Where were you anyway?"

"Rome and I had some more business to take care of. I went down to the square to meet him and—"

"Rome—," Kay interrupted her. "Rome, that's an utterly delicious name." Kay's normal contralto voice soared. "It's interesting—romantic, and Italian I'd guess."

"Well, your guess is wrong. Rome is a different name for a person all right, but in this case it has nothing at all to do with Italy. Truth is this guy is Scottish. His name is Rome Douglas. Who knows, he may be a descendant of the famous Black Douglas."

"Oh, that's fabulous. It's like that stupendous movie, *Braveheart*. All those Scottish warriors and their valiant deeds—"

"For heaven's sake get real, Kay. I don't know thing one about Rome's ancestors. And don't you fabricate some romantic background for him either." A note of exasperation edged Abby's words.

"Well then tell me everything you do know. I want to hear all about this fantastic movie they're going to make, and about them using your house. That is so great. Think of having big-name movie stars right here in Lindenwood. And Abby, you'll be right in the middle of it all. I even heard you might have a bit part or something. Is that actually so? You've just got to tell me every last detail about all of this."

Kay's rapid-fire bombardment of words clacked like castanets in Abby's ears. "Hey, put a lid on it for a second," Abby said, giving Kay a shove forward.

"I've got coffee made. Let's go to the kitchen where we can sit down and talk slow and easy over coffee and a bagel."

"I'm sorry," Kay said, giving her friend an apologetic smile. "Joe says I run off at the mouth, and I guess he's right. It's just that having a movie made here is about the most exciting thing that's ever happened. Everybody is talking about it, and I know every woman in town is green with envy because they're using your house and you get to have a firsthand part in all that goes on. I admit it. I'm jealous of that too."

"Well don't be. It has its drawbacks."

"I can't see how," Kay countered wryly.

They had reached the kitchen and Abby steered Kay to one of the rush-seated ladder-back chairs at one side of the Pembroke breakfast table. "Let me get our coffee and I'll tell you," Abby said as she took two coffee mugs from the cupboard. She also took a jar of jelly and a small package of cream cheese from the refrigerator, along with a carton of bagels. "To begin with, I let Rome talk me into letting his studio use my house against my better judgment. I really didn't want to do it."

"Why not?"

"It's inconvenient for one thing. I have to move my shop out of the house for another. More than anything, I just don't like the idea of a lot of strange people being all over my home. I even thought about backing out of the deal.'' Abby fingered the handle of her coffee mug as she as spoke, avoiding looking at Kay.

''But you're not going to, are you?'' Kay's voice escalated in alarm.

Abby gave a negative nod. ''No. Because I want the money. I need it in order to convert the carriage house into the ideal shop for my antiques. With what they're paying me, I can do that and more.''

''Joe says every business in town is going to make money out of this. It's by way of a bonanza for Lindenwood.''

''I don't doubt it,'' Abby said, spreading cream cheese on a bagel and then topping it with a spoonful of jam. ''You want to try this?'' she asked, offering it to Kay.

''You keep it, I'll fix one without the jelly. I'm trying to cut down on sweets. You're lucky to be tall and slender. An extra pound won't show on you. But every last ounce makes a bulge on you when you're five foot two and already have every curve padded,'' she said with a self-disparaging laugh. ''But now let's get back to the interesting subject of this Rome Douglas. Joe said he was very attentive, hardly took his eyes off you all through your dinner.''

''It was a business dinner after all. Rome was attentive because we were working out some details of the studio contract he wanted me to sign. That's all there was to it. So get that silly gleam out of your eye.

The only interest Rome has in me is securing the right to film his movie in Hampton House.'' Having given Kay this logical explanation, Abby took a large bite of her bagel, savoring both its aroma and its taste.

"Maybe that's his main interest at the moment. But you have to admit the present situation is fraught with romantic possibilities.'' Kay had one of those all-knowing looks in her eyes.

Abby glared back at her. "No it isn't,'' she stated adamantly.

"Of course it is—unless . . .'' Kay looked dismayed. "Oh golly, don't tell me he's married.''

"No, but—''

"Then there are no buts. You and he will be thrown together all the time while they're making this picture, and that's enough time to make anything you desire happen.''

"That's exactly the point, Kay. I don't desire anything at all to happen.''

"Oh loosen up, Abby. What's the harm in a brief little summer romance?''

"There's no future in it, that's what,'' Abby quipped. "I'm waiting for that man for all seasons, the one who'll be there for the long haul.'' She got up from the table as she declared this and poured them both some more coffee. "Now let me tell you about this great location where I'll have my antique shop while they're filming the movie.'' She artfully changed the subject of conversation, launching into a detailed account of the one vacant store only a block away from the town square that was in an ideal location and exactly the right size to house her antiques.

Rome had told Abby that he and Brent would be at her house around mid morning for Brent to take more pictures of the furnishings in the downstairs rooms. While he was doing that, Rome would be making some measurements in order to do scale drawings of the sets for the indoor scenes that would be filmed in Hampton House.

Abby hoped that Kay would be gone by then, but as luck would have it, she was just leaving as Rome and Brent arrived. Abby quickly made the introductions, inwardly praying that Kay would refrain from making any of her cute or inane remarks. Fortunately, before Kay could say anything, Rome gave her his most charming smile. "It's nice to meet you, Kay. Abby mentioned you when we saw your husband at the Foxglove the other night."

Kay's steady gaze appraised him and beamed approval. "Yes, Joe mentioned seeing Abby there with you. We're all excited about having a movie made here, you know. Perhaps Joe and I will have an opportunity to see more of you while you're here."

"We'll certainly arrange to do that, won't we Abby?" Rome glanced at Abby, the slightest flicker of a wink in his knowing look. Then, as she closed the front door after Kay left, Rome continued. "I'm curious to find out more about your matchmaking friend. Tell me, has she picked out someone to pair me off with yet?''

''What makes you think we even discussed you?'' she said with a wry smile.

''Well, didn't you?'' he asked.

She shrugged. ''Your name was mentioned. When Kay heard that it was Rome, she figured you might be Italian.''

''You're kidding me, aren't you.''

''No.'' She shook her head at him, and there was a mischievous glint in her eyes. ''But she was captivated to learn that you were not only Scottish, but might be a descendant of Douglas the Good, also called Black Douglas, who joined Robert the First and fought at Bannockburn.''

Rome stared at her in wonder. ''Are you telling me that you recall enough Scottish history from your school days that you could come up with all of that?''

''Not exactly,'' she said evasively.

His eyes now studied her with a curious intensity. ''Then would you tell me where all this knowledge did come from?''

Abby felt flustered by his scrutiny. So much so that she could feel heat rising to tint her cheeks. ''Actually, I had only a vague recollection. But the other night you mentioned the Douglas clan to me, so when I got home, I looked it up in the encyclopedia.''

Her answer seemed to both surprise and please him. ''I'm glad that you've taken this interest in the Douglas men of old,'' he said, leaning his head down closer to hers. At the same time, Rome gently touched her chin, tilting her face up so he could gaze directly into her eyes. ''Do you think it would be possible for you to show that same interest in a present-day Douglas clansman?''

Rome's face was so close to hers that Abby felt the warmth of his breath as he spoke, and he projected energy and power that undeniably attracted her. She cleared her throat, pretending not to be affected. ''I—I think I might,'' she answered, her cheeks coloring under the heat of his gaze. ''I could try.'' A reflective smile touched her lips.

''You be sure and do that, Abby.'' Rome brushed a kiss across her forehead, a kiss as tender and light as a summer breeze.

She waited until her quickened pulse subsided. Then she stepped back away from him. ''I imagine Brent has everything ready to take those pictures you want. He's probably wondering what's happened to us,'' she said, brushing her words with laughter that was fluid and feminine.

''He's not the only one. I'm wondering that too . . .'' Rome's husky laugh was sensuous and masculine.

Chapter Five

During the week that followed, Abby was busy packing up her antiques and moving them from Hampton House to the new shop location in the center of town. Both Rome and Brent assisted with the actual move. With their help, she had her new shop in order and everything all set by late in the day Friday. To show her gratitude, she wanted to take Rome and Brent out to dinner when they'd finished up, but Brent explained that he was heading home to Hollywood to spend the time that remained before the actual filming of *A Different Drummer* began with his wife and his eight- and ten-year-old sons. Rome had to turn down her invitation too, because he was driving Brent to another town, where he would catch the plane.

So it turned out that Abby just stopped, picked up a pizza, and went home to eat a solitary dinner. She ate at the kitchen table, where she could look out and see the moon soar slowly through the branches of the huge old mulberry tree, and then sail unencumbered into the dark blue heavens, attended by the stars. Abby had always found the moonlight romantic, but tonight it turned her melancholy. It suddenly occurred to her to wonder why. True, she had wanted to do something nice for Rome and Brent in return for all the help they'd given her this week. It hadn't worked out, but that was hardly reason enough for her to act like a gloomy Gus. There was a flip side to the coin. Rome wasn't going back to California with Brent. He could have, maybe he even should have, but instead, he had elected to spend this brief interlude before the filming started right here in Lindenwood. What if his reason for staying had something to do with her? That idea was appealing. Her gloom lifted.

Gazing out the window again, she observed that the moon was at its highest now, flooding sky and earth with a radiance so concentrated that you could almost hear it hum. . . .

Abby had just switched off the television and gone upstairs to get ready for bed when the telephone rang.

''I'm sorry to be calling this late, but I just got back. I hope you were still up, because I want to tell you about our agenda.'' Rome's voice sounded apologetic on the one hand and eager and determined on the other.

''It's okay. I was still up. I got hooked on a late movie on T.V. that just ended five minutes ago.'' She paused to yawn and give a sleepy sigh. ''Did you get Brent off all right?'' she asked.

''Yeah, pretty much on time too. But after that I stopped at that restaurant in North Woodstock that you told me about. You know, the one in the restored train station.''

''What did you think of it?''

''I liked it. It's rather unique. I wish you'd been there with me, but while I was eating alone I planned all the places I want to see with you during these free days I have before the Hollywood gang starts arriving next weekend.''

''Is that the agenda you mentioned?'' Her voice brightened with interest, hearing that Rome's plans included her.

''You bet, and it's gonna be a full one. We're going to Loon Mountain, Lost River, Franconia Notch, and as many other scenic spots as we can crowd into our days.''

Abby laughed. ''Apparently you've been reading the New Hampshire tour books.''

''That I have. I've read up on all the tourist attractions, and I want a bona fide New Hampshire native to be my guide to every one of them,'' he stated with enthusiasm. ''So, will you?''

''Well, it does sound like fun, Rome, but—'' She hesitated. ''I planned the opening of my newly located antique shop for this week.''

''Put it off, Abby. Can't you do that for me— please?'' There was a note of entreaty in his voice. ''There will be plenty of time for you to keep shop once the filming starts. Won't you give me all your time for this week?''

"I'd like to, but I'm not sure. Just let me sleep on it."

"Okay, but you can't sleep late," he told her emphatically. "Because, you see, I'm picking you up at nine o'clock sharp tomorrow morning. For you and I are going to drive over to Franconia for the Pollyanna Festival Parade and the hot air balloons. What do you think of that?"

"I think that I'm being strong-armed by a fast-talking Scotsman, that's what," she answered, barely able to keep the laughter from her voice. . . .

The month of July is the warmest month of summer in the White Mountains, with the temperature rising into the eighties in the daytime. The now green mountains are covered with an abundance of wildflowers, and the birds hide in the deep, cool woods, coming out only as the sun lowers, and then singing their hearts out until nightfall. In fact, late at night it's not unusual to hear an owl call.

The sunlight was warm and golden the next morning as Rome and Abby drove along the birch- and maple-lined mountain roads, wending their way north through the notches, each curve offering a surprise vista or a glimpse of a silvery pond or stream. They arrived in Franconia to find it literally teeming with happy, noisy, summer tourists. Abby soon discovered that Rome intended to take in every event, and see

every sight. Abby went along with his vigorous
agenda until well past noon. Then she called a halt.

"We've got to take a lunch break or I may faint
from hunger," she announced, placing a restraining
hand on Rome's arm. "And there's quite a renowned
place not far from here that you must experience. Believe me, they serve pancakes that are to die for. And
with them you get corncob-smoked bacon and ham
and their own country sausage that has to be the best
in the world." Her voice crescendoed with each item.

"You don't have to twist my arm," Rome said, his
smile broadening in approval. "Let's be on our way."

It took them only a short time to drive the little
distance to Polly's Pancake Parlor. The unique restaurant was in an 1830-vintage building on Hildex Farm.
Originally the structure was used as a carriage shed,
but in the 1930s it was converted into a quaint tea-
room. It has always been a family-owned operation,
and down through the years the dining room size has
been increased three times. Abby related all this his-
torical background to Rome when they arrived at the
Hildex Maple Sugar Farm. "The interesting thing is
that the home and farm have been continuously occupied by the same family (through marriage) since
the beginning."

Rome quirked an eyebrow questioningly. "And I
suppose you're going to tell me that they were all
named Polly."

Seeing the amusement in Rome's eyes, Abby made
a face at him. "Listen here, wise guy. You asked for

a native New Hampshire guide, remember? You want the guide, you get the spiel. Take it or leave it!''

''I'll sure take it,'' Rome declared emphatically, looping his arm through hers as they walked up to the door of the Pancake Parlor.

Abby glanced up at him and laughter flickered in his eyes as they met hers. She realized she enjoyed their gentle sparring as much as he did. More than that, she loved his easy camaraderie and his subtle wit.

After their lunch, they spent the rest of the afternoon visiting a gem of a small museum at Sugar Hill, and then made a brief stop at the Robert Frost Farm to view the displays pertaining to the poet and his writings.

They left the hillside farm and drove back to Lindenwood through New England's scenic byways. It was getting on to twilight and the mountains and forests were still. They heard only the muted birdsong and those furtive, mysterious stirrings about that indicated nonhuman life. At one spot a pheasant emerged, glanced an alarmed black-circled eye at them, and then scuttled back into the woods. As the dusk deepened, a deer leaped across the road, its front hooves curled close to its breast, turning its head to look at them fleetingly as it sailed by as noiseless as an apparition.

''That was an incredible sight,'' Abby cried out in delight. ''She was beautiful—a real live Bambi.''

''That's right,'' Rome agreed. ''And just think what

Brent would give to have caught that on film for one of the outdoor scenes in *A Different Drummer*."

Abby bobbed her head in agreement. "That would be something all right." She sighed, then hunched her shoulders in a despairing gesture. "It was so unexpected and happened so fast that unless he'd had his film rolling even Brent might not have been able to capture the expression in the eyes and the graceful movement of that beautiful creature."

"He'd have sure liked to try though," Rome murmured, his voice low and quiet as if he were talking more to himself than to her.

The sky in the afterglow of sunset was streaked in long scarves of coral. Clouds were gathered now in the west. They lay piled beyond the horizon, threaded with shafts of gold and pink light, but gradually even these last shreds of light filtered away, and the clouds turned black, and in the east a little new moon, like an eyelash, floated into the sky.

"You know, I owe you a dinner from last night," Abby announced as they arrived back in Lindenwood. "So would you like to collect and stop at Zeke's Fish and Steak House on the far side of the town square?"

Rome shook his head. "That sounds like a big meal, and after all that good ham and pancakes that we had at Polly's Parlor, I'm in the mood for something else. Can you guess what I'd really like to eat and where?" He gave her a boyish grin.

"No, but I expect you're going to tell me." She grinned back at him.

"Well, I'd like to stop and pick up some good Chinese carryout, and go back to your house and eat with you in your cozy, comfortable kitchen. Would that be okay?"

"Sounds good to me. I even have some fancy tea to go with it. And if you're adventuresome, I do something oriental with pears and ginger that goes great with Chinese food."

Rome's eyes swept over her approvingly. "You're just full of delightful surprises, Abby Hampton. Did you know that?"

"No, I didn't know that."

"Well you are—and don't try to tell me that nobody has never told you that before."

"If they have, I guess I don't recall who it was or why they said it." Her eyes widened with false innocence. "But I'd bet it wasn't because I offered them ginger pears." Her eyes sparkled as though she were playing a game.

"Hey, the surprises I'm talking about are lots more than that. It was just my way of saying that you're special, and I'm finding that I enjoy every single minute I spend with you. I know it may be a cliché, but— you light up my life, Abby."

Totally amazed to hear him say this, she didn't even attempt to speak. She simply looked up into his very handsome, very serious face and realized she felt much the same way about him. At that moment, she wondered if she could possibly be falling in love with Rome Douglas.

Chapter Six

Abby unlocked her front door, holding it open for Rome, since his hands were occupied with five cartons of Chinese carryout. Rome had already driven into the drive before Abby remembered the mail, so now she turned back. "I've got to run out to the street and get the mail out of the box," she told Rome. "You go on in and take the food into the kitchen."

"No, wait. It's too dark out there. I'll go get it for you, but first you get the lights on in the house while I deposit the food."

Abby was glad to let Rome take over. She quickly switched on some outside lights as well as the hall light and two lamps in the living room. Then she went to the kitchen, turned on the oven to low, and set the cartons inside so the food would stay warm while she made the tea. At this point, Rome came hurrying back inside.

"You got a magazine and several letters," he said, handing her mail to her. "Better sit down and look at it. You may have something important."

"This is my antiques magazine, which I love, and I'll pore over it later. The rest is probably junk mail."

She shuffled the three envelopes, quickly casting two aside. The third she opened, and as she unfolded the single sheet, a narrow piece of paper fell out. Abby scarcely noticed it fall to the floor, because now her eyes caught sight of the signature, and she let out a shocked gasp of surprise.

Rome had been standing at the sink washing his hands. He swung around and looked at her. "What is it Abby? Is it bad news?"

Abby didn't answer. She just stood there staring at the bold, masculine handwriting.

"You look like you've seen a ghost." Rome walked over to her, leaned down, and picked up the paper she'd dropped. "Can't be a bad ghost though. Because look, he sent you a check," he said, as he handed it to her.

Abby's hand trembled as she took it, and she found it hard to believe her eyes. But there it was. After four long years, she was actually holding in her hand Drew's check for one thousand dollars. At this late date he'd finally gotten around to paying her back the money he owed her. And it wasn't difficult to figure out why. Now that he was to be in a movie filmed in her house, he was running scared. He was afraid she'd blow the whistle on him, tell the Allied crew what a fraud and four-flushing cad he truly was. She tossed her head and gave a contemptuous chuckle. "Well, what do you know? It was a long time coming, but this deadbeat ghost has decided it's to his advantage to finally pay his honest debt. And guess what? It's all because of *A Different Drummer.*'' Her voice was marble-cold and brittle as ice, but there was a gleam of satisfaction shining in her eyes.

Rome studied her face, his eyes narrowed in a questioning frown. ''I can't possibly figure how our Allied film could enter into this, but I'd be interested to know, if you care to tell me.''

Abby lowered her head to escape Rome's curious gaze. She busied her still shaky fingers by folding the check and the letter and stuffing them back in the envelope. Then she crossed to the kitchen and stuck the envelope on the refrigerator door, securing it with a decorative daisy magnet. ''It's not really all that interesting a story, Rome. I'd just as soon forget it, if you don't mind.''

He had followed after her and stood behind her, letting his hands rest lightly on her shoulders. ''Okay, whatever you say. But I want you to know I'm a good listener. Any time you need to talk about anything, I'm here for you.'' He gently kneaded her shoulders as he spoke, then he turned her around to face him, taking her into his arms. For a brief moment he seemed to kiss her with his eyes. A second later, his lips slowly descended to meet hers. His kiss was slow and thoughtful, and his lips were warm and sweet and more persuasive than she cared to admit. She was shocked by her own eager response. Abby had no desire to back out of his embrace, but at last, reluctantly, she put her hands on Rome's chest and eased herself from his arms. "I'm feeling light-headed," she said. "Must be from hunger." Abby spoke with as reasonable a voice as she could manage, casting her eyes downward to mask the emotions she was feeling from Rome's probing gaze.

"I'm dizzy too," Rome said huskily, "but it has nothing at all to do with food. It's far more exciting than that!" His eyes moved over her with open approval.

Abby took a frank and admiring look back at him. "I can't argue with that, Rome." There was a trace of laughter in Abby's voice.

Rome studied her with caring eyes. Then he laughed too, and his laughter was full-hearted and triumphant.

Abby agreed to go along with the agenda of activities that Rome had mapped out for them on both Monday and Tuesday, but she insisted that for the latter part of the week she must have her shop open. "I can't afford not to. The summer tourist trade is a large part of my business," she explained. "You can understand that, can't you?"

Rome admitted that he understood, but just didn't like it. However, he agreed, on the condition that Abby would allow him to spend those afternoons in the shop helping out, after which she'd go to dinner with him at the various interesting restaurants in Lindenwood and nearby Lincoln and Woodstock. She most happily consented to that plan.

Rome surprised her on Monday when he announced that he'd managed to get two tickets for tonight's summer theater players performance of *Man of La Mancha*.

Abby was amazed. "I was told they were sold out for every performance. How did you manage to get a pair of seats?"

"You know how it is. They claim there's standing room only, but they'll always find a good seat or two for a certain kind of people."

"What certain kind is that?" she asked, eyeing him curiously.

He cocked his head at her, a knowing look in his eyes and a detached smile about his lips. "Oh, people like New York theater critics and movie talent scouts from Hollywood."

She frowned. "But you're neither one of those." She planted her hands on her hips and gave him an arch look.

He chuckled. "No I'm not, but they think I might be."

"And just what did you do to make them think that, smart guy?" She cocked her head at him, copying his expression to mock him.

"I let it slip that I was with Allied Studios and that

we were here on location for our next film. They just assume what they will about what my job entails.''

''Tell me, do all Scotsmen play such tricky little games?''

''Only when it'll get them two third row center seats,'' he told her with a self-satisfied expression marking his face.

''I have to commend you, Rome.'' She gave him a delicious smile. ''You Scotsmen are wonderfully resourceful.'' Her eyes were bright with merriment.

Knowing Rome had gone to considerable trouble to make the evening special, Abby dressed in her most becoming summer outfit, a white, silk-linen sheath dress with a rainbow-colored bolero jacket. They went to the picturesque Sea Shell restaurant, a place that claimed it served only the freshest seafood from New England ports, for dinner. Then, not wanting to be late for the eight o'clock curtain, they skipped dessert, postponing it for later, after the play.

They were wise to have done this, for they got settled in their choice, third row center seats, and had just enough time to glance briefly at the playbill when the lights dimmed in warning, then brightened again. A final rush of people came down the aisles now, hurrying to find their places. The lights dimmed once more. This time a hush settled over the audience, and the ôrchestra began playing the overture. Then, as the footlights glowed and the curtain rose, revealing the first act stage set, Rome leaned over and whispered in her ear, "I hope to get the chance to design sets for a Broadway theater production sometime."

Even though he'd spoken in a hushed tone, Abby sensed he felt strongly about it. Possibly even it was a major career goal he desired to achieve. It gave her a special feeling to think that he'd wanted to share this personal dream of his with her. She wanted to tell him this, but she couldn't, for the actors had come on the stage and the opening lines were being spoken.

It was a memorable play, and Abby was still humming the melody of the final song as she and Rome left the theater. As they walked to the car, the night was fragrant all about them, and a canopy of small stars shone high above. The hour was late and there was little traffic. The tall post lamps threw a soft line of light along the streets, but there was no longer light behind the windows of the houses they passed.

"It was a wonderful evening, Rome. I enjoyed every minute of it," Abby said, as Rome took her to her door.

"Me too. But then that goes without saying, because I like every bit of time I spend with you." He looked at her, some private emotion glistening in his eyes.

"I'm glad you said it though." Abby's smile was lovely and open, illuminating her face.

She watched his eyes darken as he circled his arms

around her. Then he was kissing her and it was wonderfully intoxicating for a few precious moments. When the moments were over, she stood there looking up at him. The night was very still around them.

A smile touched Rome's mouth with sensual warmth, the sight of which made Abby's heart turn over. "Good night," he said softly.

She echoed his good night, watching after him as he turned and walked away.

Chapter Seven

Abby opened her eyes. The first lightening of dawn was beginning to creep through the windows of her bedroom. The wallpaper's silver and pink satin stripes glowed in the pale light. At the window, the pink sheer curtains lapped the air slowly. Peace and stillness were part of the early dawn, with only the birds to say how quiet it was. The robins, blue jays, and a mockingbird made chirping cuts in the stillness, and there was a scurry of wings in the cedar tree.

Abby yawned and stretched, then attempted to focus her sleepy eyes on the clock on the bedside table. "Only five-thirty," she muttered to herself, thinking that that was an unthinkable hour. What would possibly cause her to wake up at dawn, especially after being out until after midnight the night before? With a sleepy moan, she turned over, nested her head deep into the down pillow, and closed her eyes to return to sleep. It was precisely at this moment that the telephone rang.

The phone was on the nightstand next to the clock. She groped for the receiver and barely managed to grab it up without knocking the clock onto the floor.

Her "hello" was one part sleepy groan and the other part irritated grumble.

"Good morning!" Rome's voice was cheerful as a lark. "I didn't wake you up, did I?" he asked in his brassy-bright tone. "It is time to rise and shine, you know."

"For heaven's sake, Rome. It's just five-thirty in the morning. I don't rise until at least seven. And as for shining, I don't manage that until about nine."

He chuckled. "Got to do better than that today. We've got to get an early start for what I've got on our agenda. In fact, we need to leave in about forty-five minutes."

"Oh my," she groaned, louder this time. "After our late night, you've got to be kidding."

"No, I'm not kidding." He sounded determined and assertive.

Well, she could be assertive too. "I'm afraid you're going to have to modify the plans, Rome. I can't be ready to go anyplace before at least eight. Where do you want to go so early anyway?"

"You remember that movie with Katharine Hepburn and Henry Fonda, *On Golden Pond*? I just learned it was filmed nearby at Squam Lake. I can't wait to drive there and see it. It's a sight I sure don't want to miss."

"And you shouldn't miss it. But it's a lake, not 'The Star-Spangled Banner,' so do we have to view it in the dawn's early light?"

He laughed. "I guess not. But humor me, won't you? Get up now and get dressed, and I'll pick you up in exactly one hour. I'll bring along a thermos of coffee and a box of doughnuts. You can eat your breakfast in the car on the way. Okay?"

"I guess so," she agreed grudgingly. "But don't expect me to be bright-eyed and charming so early in the morning."

"All right, I'll settle for dreamy-eyed and alluring."

"What you're going to get is sleepy-eyed and yawning," she told him, hanging up the phone before he could mock her further.

Abby climbed slowly out of her bed, at the moment feeling very little enthusiasm for Rome's plans for how they were going to spend this day. It took her several minutes, but she did muster up the strength to consider a brisk shower, knowing it was the only way to revive herself and make herself get a move on. When Rome said he'd be after her in one hour, he meant exactly sixty minutes.

A warm shower with herbal flower-scented soap, followed by a two-second shot of an all-cold spray, did indeed work a minor miracle on her—not just physically, but mentally too. And a careful application of a bit of makeup didn't hurt either. Apple-red lipstick and a touch of blush really does put a glow on a sleep-deprived face. Her attitude was now vastly improved.

She had a good idea that Rome would get her onto

one of the hiking or bike trails that abound throughout the White Mountains, and she had little doubt that he also had in mind canoeing on Squam Lake. With these activities on the agenda, she dressed accordingly in jeans, a white shirt with roll-up sleeves, and a comfortable, seasoned pair of jogging shoes.

Once she was dressed, she took a look at herself and decided her long slender legs in narrow-cut stovepipe jeans, and her loose-fitting man's tailored shirt made her look like Huckleberry Finn. Not an appealing thought, and certainly not an image she wanted to put in Rome's mind. She lost no time in searching through a bureau drawer to find a yellow, rose, and blue patterned scarf which she tied around her head to hold her hair back off her face. She then put on a pair of gold stud earrings. Checking her reflection in the mirror one more time, she gave a halfhearted shrug. At least she looked less like a tomboy now. She quickly gathered up a denim shoulder purse, stuffing in a comb, lipstick, and whatever she thought she should have for spending a day in the great outdoors. Recalling the possibility of Rome wanting to go boating at the lake, she figured she'd better take a sweater or a jacket. The breeze off the water could be fairly cool, even in July. She opted for the bright blue zipfront jacket she wore for jogging.

Abby had every intention of being ready and even waiting outside on the porch when Rome arrived. She would have, too, except at the last minute she couldn't remember where she'd left her dark glasses. She finally found them by the kitchen telephone about the same time that Rome's car turned into her driveway. By racing out the back door and flying through the breezeway, she managed to reach the car before Rome could turn off the motor. He saluted her with a wave and a grin, leaned over, and with his long reach swung the passenger side door open for her to hop in. Thus in a matter of seconds they were backing out the drive and heading off to spend a glorious day together on Golden Pond.

Abby couldn't help but find Rome's early-morning cheerfulness infectious. And by the time she'd eaten two sugar doughnuts and downed a cup of the coffee he'd brought for her, she felt energized and ready to rise to any occasion. It was well that she felt that way, because Rome's enthusiasm never waned. As Abby had anticipated, he wanted to engage in all the activities at the lake—except he did agree that the water was probably a bit too chilly for swimming this early in the day. "Besides, neither of us brought along our swimsuits," Abby reminded him.

"And I guess you don't go in much for skinny-dipping," he teased, giving her a wicked grin.

"You guessed exactly right about that," Abby countered, grinning back at him.

Rome had rented a boat with an outboard motor so they could cover a large area of the lake. He told Abby that he wanted to search out the scenic coves and inlets before the sun rose to the center of the sky, where its rays would reflect a shiny glare off the water. Also, there was little activity on the lake now, only a few dedicated fishermen could be spotted maneuvering row boats quietly in some of the deeply shaded and secluded parts of the lake.

The morning air was fresh and smelled seductively of the flowers and trees which scented it. When they were traveling close to the shoreline, Abby caught glimpses of dew sparkling on the reeds and bushes that grew along the lake's edge, and spiderwebs decorated the bramble bushes and shrubs with medallions of silver lace. The scenery was beautiful and everything was serene. She and Rome both enjoyed it, saying little. The silence was comfortable between them, the way it is with two people who have begun to know each other well enough that they don't have to make idle conversation.

Shortly after noon, the sun was directly overhead. Its bright rays reflected daggers of sharp light off the water and the air was filled with summer heat. "It's full speed ahead," Rome announced, wiping perspiration off his forehead with the back of his hand and pointing their boat toward the shore.

She was glad to see that there was a fast-food café near the dock where they had rented the boat. When they walked inside, the appetizing aroma of charcoal-broiled meat cooking made Abby's mouth water. Rome got them char-burgers, and french fries and onion rings and large paper cups of shaved ice, which were filled to the brim with lemon-flavored tea. Nothing had ever tasted so good before, and she doubted it could again.

Rome and Abby took it slow and easy on the drive back to Lindenwood. They were in a region where the landscape was rugged, and the mountains soared 4000 feet to the sky. It made you want to take slow, deep breaths and just drink in the beauty and tranquillity of the surroundings.

"Just a few miles from where we are now we're going to come to one of New Hampshire's historic covered bridges," Abby told him. "And before we drive through it there's something I want you to do for me, even though you'll probably think it's foolish." She had her head lowered and she stole a glance at Rome out of the corner of her eye. "Will you promise me you'll try it?"

"If it's what I think it is, I will." He sounded rather amused.

She was intrigued by his quick agreement, because she really doubted that he had any idea what she was going to ask of him. "And what do you think it is?"

"Well," he said, arching one eyebrow in a knowing look. "Though you've told me you don't go to many movies, I'm still betting that you've seen a movie called *The Bridges of Madison County* on television. And because you have, you want me to pick you a bunch of wildflowers and then take your picture standing in the opening of this historic covered bridge of yours just like Clint Eastwood did for Meryl Streep on that bridge in the movie. Am I right?''

She shook her head slowly, a mysterious Mona Lisa smile on her face. ''That's a nice thought, and a romantic thing to do, but it's not what we do in New England. There's a kind of tradition that we follow here with our bridges.''

''Are you going to tell me what it is, or shall I try another guess?''

''You can try, but I doubt you'll guess right.''

''I bet you want me to carve our initials inside the bridge.''

Abby threw up her hands in protest. ''Heavens, no! I think they could put us in jail for that. I'll have you know, Rome, we preserve our historic old bridges, not desecrate them,'' she declared with fervor.

''Hey, I'm from California, so what do I know?'' He managed to sound contrite, but there was a glint of mockery in his eyes.

''Well, obviously not much about the fifty-four historic covered bridges in this state.'' She derided him with a humorous chuckle.

''Then maybe you'd better clue me in, Smarty.'' He gave her a good-natured grin.

''Okay, I'll be happy to do that,'' she said gaily, as she shifted in her seat so she could study his profile, and monitor his expressions as she talked. She almost regretted now bringing up the subject of the covered bridges. Rome would find all this childish and see it as some sort of a foolish game she was playing with him, and she'd been silly to start it in the first place. She heaved a deep sigh. "Well, there's this sort of custom that goes along with our covered bridges. It starts when you're a kid, at least it did with me. I was told that when you come to a covered bridge, you make a wish. Then, before you start across the bridge, you take a really deep breath, and if you can hold that breath until you pass clear through to the other side of the bridge then your wish will come true." Abby paused after she said all this and waited for Rome to comment. When he didn't, she quickly added, "I was thinking that both of us could make a wish when we cross the bridge."

"You believe all of this works for you, right?" Rome inquired thoughtfully.

"I think so, but I don't really have any proof. You see, I was just a little kid the times I tried it, and I just couldn't hold my breath long enough to get clear across a bridge."

"But you think I could do it?"

"Yeah, I'm sure you could if you really tried. But you have to wish for something really important, you know. It's got to be something you want a whole lot." She spoke deliberately, and her expression was totally serious.

He turned his head to look at her closely. "Will you

be wishing for something important too?'' he asked, his voice and manner as serious as hers.

She bobbed her head. ''Of course,'' she said emphatically. ''My wish is about something that affects both of us in a way.''

It was obvious that her response not only interested Rome, but greatly intrigued him. ''Like what?'' he asked curiously. ''And how?''

''I can't tell you now. That could ruin it.'' She shook her head emphatically. ''But if I can hold my breath and make it through the bridge, I'll tell you then. Is that a deal?'' She held out her hand to him.

Rome took his hand off the steering wheel long enough to grasp hers and give it a confirming shake. ''That's a deal,'' he said warmly.

In only a few more minutes they were at the quaint old covered bridge that spanned the Pemigewasset River. ''Okay,'' Abby said. ''This is it.''

Rome slowed the car to a crawl. ''Wow, it looks like a fairly long bridge.''

''You better believe it. So don't take too long to drive us across.''

''Don't panic, Abby. It's a piece of cake.'' He gave her a reassuring wink. ''You all set?''

She nodded, then took a mammoth breath as they drove into the shadowy and silent interior of the bridge. This wasn't any snap for Abby. The moments seemed to drag by, and she barely managed to hold on until the car nosed out into the sunlight at the other end. In that split second she let out her breath in a gasp and avidly gulped in fresh air.

Rome noisily inhaled a fresh breath too. "That was a slight challenge at that," he admitted, thrusting his chin at a proud angle. "Now I can say—been there, done that," he added with a chuckle.

"Me too. But I was afraid there right near the last that I might not make it."

"We both made it, and we both get our wish," Rome said, taking her hand and giving it a victory squeeze. "So now, tell me your wish."

"Well, it has to do with something you told me last night at the play."

He frowned. "Oh, what did I say?" He sounded puzzled.

"It was about wanting someday to design the sets for a Broadway play."

"Yeah, that's something I really hope to get the opportunity to do in the next year or two." He fingered the leather-wrapped steering wheel absently, his eyes narrowed, a thoughtful expression on his face. "I've been thinking about it a lot lately, for some reason. Probably because of being around here, where there's lots of theater work being done."

"I had a feeling when you told me about it, that it was important to you. I guess that's why I wished that you'd be offered the chance to do it."

"Is that the only reason," he asked, glancing over at her.

"What other reason would there be?"

A speculative smile played across his lips. "Oh, I thought the fact that I'd then be working in New York, rather than Hollywood, which would mean we could see each other fairly often just might figure into it." A smile now danced in his expressive eyes. "Did you ever think of that?"

Abby tipped her head and gave Rome a sidelong glance, her full curved lips pursed meditatively. "Now that you mention it, that thought did enter my mind," she said sweetly.

"I could kiss you for that, Abby."

"Not while you're driving you couldn't," she countered, laughing.

Instantly Rome braked the car and pulled off onto the shoulder.

"What are you doing?" she asked, still laughing.

"What do you think?" he said, quickly silencing her laughter with a thoroughly enjoyable kiss.

Chapter Eight

Abby opened her shop downtown on Wednesday morning. She had set a sign at Hampton House beside her mailbox notifying her customers of her new location. Besides doing this, she had also had flyers printed which she delivered to the White Mountains Tourist Center, where hopefully they would be picked up by the summer tourists. This, plus word of mouth she hoped, would be all she needed to get her new shop off and running.

Her first day was a bit slow, and only a handful of browsers came during the morning. By mid afternoon, however, the numbers picked up, and she made a few modest sales. Thursday was a different story. A chartered bus full of retired civil service workers arrived for lunch and two hours of sight-seeing and shopping. No sooner had they left Lindenwood when several groups of musicians began to filter in. These colorful bands were beginning to gather in the area for the Bluegrass Festival that's held in July. There was almost steady traffic in and out of Abby's shop. She made a surprising number of rather large sales in both cut glass and Dresden figurines. One man bought two of her more unique paperweights, and at the end of the afternoon she was holding the door open for her last customer to carry out a large carton which held a very pricey Tiffany glass lamp.

It was now getting close to six o'clock. With a weary but contented sigh, Abby walked over to turn the sign in the corner of the front window from OPEN to CLOSED. Rome had told her that he'd either be at the shop at six, or if he got detained, he'd telephone for her to meet him at Zeke's restaurant on the town square. She began checking around to make sure she was leaving everything in order. A few minutes later, she was just finishing placing the money from the cash drawer into the steel safe located in the storage area at the back, when she heard the bell tinkle, which indicated that someone had entered the front door. She expected it to be Rome. "I'll be there in a minute," she called, twirling the dial on the safe and heading toward the front again.

The moment she glimpsed the man, she knew it wasn't Rome. He wasn't nearly as tall, in fact he was of medium build and only average height. The fellow had his back to Abby and was examining something in the front showcase. He didn't turn around, so she spoke again as she came within a few feet of him. "I'm already closed for the day, but if you're interested in seeing something in the case, I'd be happy to take it out for you," she said politely.

The young man spun around, rushing to her and

grabbing her up in an enthusiastic bear hug. "Surprise, surprise," he yelled, twirling her around. "I just got into town, Abby, and I couldn't wait to see my pretty New England pigeon. I asked at the inn where I could find Abby Hampton, then I hightailed it over here to get you so we could go have dinner and reminisce about old times."

The initial shock of what was happening literally took her breath away. It took her several seconds to register Drew's outpouring of words and come to her senses. When she did, she glared at him, pounding his chest with her fists. "Put me down this instant, you—you fool. You must be crazy!"

"Yeah, I'm crazy. Crazy with joy at being here and seeing you," he said, laughing as he let go of her. "And don't try to act like you're not glad I'm here, because I know you are."

There was an irritating hint of arrogance about him, and she knew his attitude hadn't changed. He was still convinced that he captivated every woman he met. She met his insolent gaze and smiled benignly. "You're the actor, Drew, not I. And to be perfectly honest I have no feelings about your being here one way or the other." She lifted her chin and looked him squarely in the eye. "A Hollywood studio is paying me to let them use my house for a film. That I'm pleased about. But the actors and actresses who are to play in the movie, and all of the business and hoopla that goes with making a movie in our little town, is not my concern, nor is it of any particular interest to me.''

''Oh, come off it, Abby. You're saying that because you're still mad at me because I took so long to repay the money you loaned me. But that's all squared away and it's time to let bygones be bygones.'' He reached out for her again, but she was too fast for him. She turned on her heels, moving well out of his reach.

Apparently he didn't feel rebuffed by either her words or her attitude. He simply took a few steps toward her, then stopped, thrust his hands down in his pockets, and gave her a complaisant and charming smile. ''Come on, Abby. I'll take you to dinner and we can talk and laugh and remember all those good times we had together. You and I really do have a lot of catching up to do, you know.'' His voice was deep and unhurried and he looked at her through half-lowered lids.

Drew was a good actor, she'd have to give him that. He struck a lot of poses, but fortunately Abby was now familiar with all of them. These thoughts made her gloat inwardly, and then she looked at Drew and shook her head negatively. ''No, we really don't,'' she said, keeping her voice calm. ''You and I are truly caught up, Drew, believe me. Furthermore, I'd like to leave it that way.'' She forced her lips into a good-natured smile. ''Besides, I have a date for dinner, and he should be getting here any time now.''

The tension in Drew's jaw betrayed his frustration, but he was quick to mask it with a condescending smile. "Then we'll just have to make it tomorrow night, won't we? I'll pick you up at your place at seven."

He was so cocky, so absolutely sure of himself and his control over her. He had paid no attention to a single word she'd said. Either that, or he refused to take it seriously. He simply wouldn't believe that any woman could possibly reject him. Abby clenched her hands into fists, pressing them tight against her sides as she struggled to keep a rein on her emotions and hold down the tensions building up inside her. "No, not tomorrow—not anytime." She spoke slowly, deliberately accenting each word.

As she finished saying this, Rome came dashing through the door. "I'm a trifle late I know. I'm—" He stopped in mid sentence, evidently just then catching sight of Drew. "Excuse me, Abby, didn't realize you had a customer."

"Quite all right. He's not a customer," Abby said, immediately going to meet Rome and taking hold of his arm, a welcoming smile easing the tense lines around her mouth. "You arrived just in time to meet one of the actors in your movie. Rome, this is Drew Daniels."

"Of course, I recognize you now," Rome said, extending his hand to Drew. "They just told me at the inn that you'd checked in. You're the first.'' He shook the other man's hand warmly. ''I'm Rome Douglas, but I'm called the Scotsman,'' Rome added with a genial smile.

''Glad to meet you, Rome. I was told that the Scotsman was in charge of things here on location. And I must say I'm glad you chose this place. It gave me the chance to come back and see my friend Abby again.''

Abby cringed at this, and tightened her hold on Rome's arm. Not wanting Drew and Rome to get into any further conversation, she quickly interrupted. ''Drew, you're going to have to excuse us. Rome's made dinner reservations and we do have to go.''

Rome shot her a surprised look, but made no comment. Drew simply shrugged his shoulders and gave Rome a brief smile. ''See you around.'' He bobbed his head in a brief salute and turned to leave. ''I'll be back in touch, Pigeon. You and I really do have some major catching up to do.'' He flung these words over his shoulder as he went out the door.

''Reservations at Zeke's—that's a first,'' Rome said, laughing and circling his arm around her waist.

''Well, I needed some excuse to get rid of him, and that was all I could think of at the moment. Don't knock it. It worked, didn't it?'' Her smile was gleeful.

''I don't get it. Why didn't you tell me that you and this Drew Daniels were such old buddies.''

"Because we're not," she snapped, pulling away from him and walking behind a counter to collect her purse.

"He seems to think you are. Even had a pet name for you. *Pigeon,* wasn't that what he called you?" Rome's voice had an edge to it, and he'd wiped the smile off his face.

Abby nodded. "Not too flattering a label, but it fit me at the time, in a way." She came around to join Rome again. "Come on. Let's walk to Zeke's. If I'm going to talk about that fateful summer when I met Drew, it's not going to be on an empty stomach."

As they walked the few blocks to the restaurant, Abby was thinking about just how much she needed to tell Rome about her dealings with Drew. She was hesitant about giving him all the painful details. In the first place, she hated to let Rome know how naive and stupid she'd been. That she'd been so charmed and captivated by this handsome actor, and had so romanticized him in her mind that all reason had left her. Abby sighed as these thoughts made the same hurts and mental wounds rise out of that time gone by the way fog rises in the river bottom. She clamped her lips together in a firm line, swearing inwardly that she would never allow herself to become that vulnerable ever again.

It took only a few minutes to walk the short distance to the restaurant. They were soon settled in a back booth and once they'd told the waiter how they wanted their steaks cooked, they returned to the subject of Drew.

"I guess I could have told you that I knew Drew when you first told me he was to be in your movie. I think I did say I'd heard of him," Abby said, trying to ease into the subject of Drew in a way that Rome would see it as no big deal.

"All I remember is that you made quite a point about not being interested much in either movies or movie stars," Rome commented, leaning his back against the leather-padded booth and crossing his arms across his chest. "Naturally, I'm curious why this movie actor says he's a friend of yours from way back, and that you two have so much catching up to do."

"That's a farce, Rome. He just wants to make sure I'm not going to blow the whistle on him with all of you who are working on this movie." She gave a derisive shrug. "There's nothing for us to catch up on, and the less I see of him the better."

"You sound like you feel strongly about that."

"I do!"

A look of relief spread across Rome's face, altering his intense expression. "Well, I can't pretend I'm not glad to hear that. I was afraid Drew was someone important out of your past, and now that he had resurfaced I figured you'd dump me for this younger, better-looking hunk."

"You've got to be kidding." Abby peered at him, a look of amused speculation narrowing her eyes. "You couldn't possibly think that."

"Why not? I'm a normal man. I get jealous just like any other guy."

She leaned across the table toward him, smiling. "In the first place, you and Drew are probably within a year or two of the same age. In the second place, you're tall, handsome, well built, and let's not overlook the fact that you're a true Scotsman of the Douglas clan. I'd say that's makes you a winner." Her merry eyes were glowing.

"And I'd say that's the most out-and-out flattery I've ever been given, but don't think for a minute that I'm not plenty glad to get it," Rome said, reaching his hand across the table to her. Their eyes met, their hands touched, and they laughed. It was a fleeting moment between them; it lasted barely a second. Yet it was significant in their relationship, and they both sensed it.

As they began to eat their dinner, Abby started telling Rome about the summer she had met Drew. "You don't know this, Rome, but I'm one of those industrious New England gals. I took a job every summer while I was getting through college."

"Good for you," he said, giving her a little mock salute. "I admire anybody who can earn tuition and a year's room and board with only a summer job. Who did you work for, Chase Manhattan Bank?"

"You think you're funny, don't you?" She made a wry face. "My folks had set up a college fund that took care of that major stuff. But I did buy my clothes out of what I earned working in the summer. However, if you're not interested in hearing about what I was doing when I met Drew the summer between my junior and senior year at the university, I just won't bore you with it." She pretended to be put out with him, but there was an impish glint in her eyes.

"Look, you know I was only teasing. So please, tell me all that happened, because believe me, I'm interested."

"Okay. But remember, it's not easy for me to tell you all this. I was barely twenty, had never been west of the Mississippi, and by today's standards had led a relatively sheltered life. So judge me accordingly, please."

Rome smiled reassuringly. "I'm not going to judge you at all, Abby."

"Good," she answered, a trace of a smile touching her lips. "That particular summer I got a job in a gift and craft shop at Loon Mountain. Drew was one of the actors in a theater company that was performing there that summer. From the moment he got there, he spread his charm all over the place. In no time he had every young girl, middle-aged matron, and elderly lady entranced. And, of course, all the unattached cuties hovered near the theater for a chance to gain some special attention from him.'' She paused long enough to spread butter on her last bite of roll.

Rome watched her, his expression placid. ''What about you? Did you hover?''

''Oh, I thought he was good-looking and all that, and I wasn't exactly immune to that practiced charm he passed out. But I'm tall and leggy and more the girl-next-door type than a cute little groupie. So no—I didn't hover.'' She stopped talking long enough to eat her roll. Rome waited for her to continue with her story, a detached smile about his lips.

Abby took a drink of her iced tea, eyeing Rome over the edge of her glass suspiciously. ''Whatever you're thinking, go on and say it.''

''Only that a tall, slender, beautiful girl-next-door type sounds perfect to me. What did our hotshot actor think of her?''

''That's a good question.'' Abby gave a caustic laugh. ''I'll tell you the rest of the story and you can judge for yourself.'' She took another drink of her tea before setting her glass down and continuing. ''Drew came into the shop where I worked fairly often during the first couple of weeks. Soon he was dropping in regularly, often two or three times a day. From the beginning he called me a shy little New England pigeon. Said I was neat and soft as a puff of smoke and quiet as a moonbeam. I thought how romantic he was to talk like that. Probably the truth is that he was just stealing lines from one of his plays." She made a scoffing sound. "I sure got taken in by that phony. Every time I think about how he conned me, I want to scream. I'm no longer soft or quiet, and I defy anyone to call me *pigeon* again." Abby's voice crescendoed with each word. Suddenly she realized that the people at the tables near their booth were looking at her. She covered her mouth with her hands and tried to hide by moving farther into the corner of her side of the booth. "Do you think everybody heard me?" she whispered, her face pink with embarrassment.

"Only those within a ten-foot radius," Rome answered, a hint of laughter surrounding his words.

"Oh wow! That takes in everything but the kitchen and the front cashier's counter," Abby groaned, her rosy flush spreading now along her neck. "We're just going to have to eat slow and wait until most of them are gone. I'm certainly not going to walk out of here and let everyone see who it was that said all those things."

Rome looked like he was having a hard time restraining an amused grin. "We can do that if you really want to, Abby. But I think I should point out that Zeke's regulars are all familiar Lindenwood folks, and they all know you. I rather expect that they've already figured out who it was."

"Gee. Thanks for pointing that out to me, Rome." She made a face at him.

"You know, it wasn't all that bad."

"That's easy for you to say." She was still cowering in the corner of the booth.

"Come on, forget it. Tell me the rest about Drew."

"All right, but you're going to have to listen closely. I'm not speaking above a whisper from here on out."

Rome put his elbow on the table and leaned forward. "Go ahead, I'm all ears."

"And don't make any more fun of me." She mouthed her words broadly in a subdued voice.

"I wouldn't dare," he answered, mimicking her manner.

"Well, for the rest of the summer everything between Drew and me went swimmingly. Everything was fun and exciting. There were several other girls from the university working in the shops and restaurants at Loon Mountain. But I was the one that was getting all of Drew's attention. He was the star attraction and he picked me out. That was kinda heady stuff for a girl-next-door type. You can see that, can't you?"

"No, and I don't even want to try," he said, scowling at her. "Just tell me what feat this big leading man pulled off next."

"He set the stage to play his really big scene, that's what he did. It was in August, and the theater company was performing the final play of the summer season. Drew was approached by a talent scout from one of the Hollywood movie studios. He was to go to California for a screen test as soon as the play closed. Of course he saw this as his great opportunity and was convinced that he'd make it big if only he arrived in Hollywood with everything going for him, the impeccably tailored suit, expensive shoes, all the right accoutrements to make that important first impression. That's when he asked me to loan him one thousand dollars.''

''He had the nerve to ask a college girl he'd known for only a couple of months for that amount of money? Where did he expect you to get it?''

''That's exactly what I asked him. I didn't have any money.'' She threw out her hands, palms up. ''I had a trust fund that paid my college tuition and living expenses. All I ever had in cash was a very modest monthly allowance.''

''What did Drew say when you told him that?'' Rome asked curiously.

''He was appalled. I remember that he got red in the face as if he was really angry for a few seconds. He acted so odd in fact that I probably should have guessed that he'd go to extreme measures to get the money he wanted.''

Rome was studying Abby closely as she related this, a frown of conjecture wrinkling the bridge of his nose. ''And did he? Go to extremes I mean?''

''From my point of view he did. Although it took me a while to find that out.''

"What do you mean?"

"Four or five days after he'd first asked me to loan him the money, he came to me with what he said was the perfect solution. He said he'd talked to an antique dealer in Concord who would loan him the money if we put up an antique of the same value. He would then hold the antique for ninety days, at which time I could reclaim it. Of course, Drew said he knew he could repay me the thousand dollars within ninety days, so I would be under no risk at all. This way he'd have the money he needed to go for his screen test, and he'd repay me in time to reclaim my antique. He repeated this to me a number of times, and though I really didn't want to do it, he made it sound so reasonable and easy that I agreed." She paused, absently chewing at the corner of her lip, a pained expression on her face. "I made a stupid, foolish mistake. One that I've regretted every day since."

"I'm curious about what it was Drew gave the dealer in Concord. You didn't have your antique shop that many years ago."

"No, but I had Hampton House and all the family heirlooms. I naturally expected to use a piece of furniture or the grandfather clock in the entry. The value of fine old furniture is fairly well established. I knew of several items that would be acceptable. But Drew had a specific thing he insisted upon. It was a porcelain clock that belonged to my grandmother Abigail, for whom I was named. It was a table clock, so not extremely large. Drew said it would be easier to take that to Concord. He could do that himself. A piece of furniture might have to be crated and sent down by truck.''

''I guess that did make sense. But from your tone of voice I guess you really didn't want him to take that clock.''

She sighed and closed her eyes for a moment, squeezing back the sudden moisture that filled her eyes. ''No, I didn't. I loved that clock. It had special meaning for me because of my grandmother. And of all the things I inherited when I got Hampton House, the one thing I never wanted to part with was that clock.''

Rome frowned. ''But you got it back in ninety days didn't you? Drew did pay you back when he got the movie contract, surely.''

Abby's expression was one of mute wretchedness. ''I never heard a single word from Drew after he left here that summer. He didn't call, he didn't write—and he certainly didn't repay me in ninety days. In fact, it took him four years before he finally got around to doing that.''

Rome stared at her in astonishment. ''You mean that was Drew's check that fell out of that letter just the other night?'' Rome's voice echoed his surprise.

''That was it.'' She gave a scoffing laugh. ''And after all this time the only reason he would pay me back at all is that he's running scared. He's so afraid that I'll tell all the people he's going to be working with on this picture just what a sorry character he really is. That's why he's making this grandstand play, acting like we're such tried and true, dear old friends— and all that ballyhoo.''

"That guy is a real piece of work." Rome spat out the words contemptuously. "I can understand now why you don't want to have anything further to do with him." He reached out his hand and covered hers where it rested on the table. "I'm going to make it my business to shield you from him during the filming if that's okay with you," he said gently.

Abby nodded. "I don't know what you can do, but I'd appreciate seeing as little of him as possible."

"I'll take care of it." He squeezed her hand reassuringly. "Now I want to know about your grandmother's clock. What's happened with it?"

"That's the part of this whole story that paints the true picture of Drew Daniels." Abby's voice was quiet, yet held an undertone of animosity. "You see, there never was a chance that I would get it back. Drew lied about that from the start. He didn't have any ninety-day agreement with the antique dealer. That was just a story he concocted so I'd let him take my clock."

"Are you telling me that Drew just sold your clock outright?" Rome's expression clouded in anger.

Abby nodded. "Yes, and for twelve hundred dollars."

"How did you find that out? And when?"

"When I hadn't heard from Drew after ninety days, I went down to Concord to contact the dealer, to see if he'd hold the clock a little longer and let me pay back the thousand dollars in monthly payments of two hundred dollars. When I told him all this, he just stared at me, obviously totally bewildered by my story. Then, of course, he told me the real story—that Drew had appeared in his shop wanting to sell him this clock for fifteen hundred dollars. The dealer said he offered Drew twelve hundred and Drew took it. That was the moment when I had to face up to the fact that I had been very thoroughly taken, and that Drew Daniels was a liar, a cheat, and the most unscrupulous person I've ever known." Abby's face had paled with anger as she related all of this to Rome, and she seethed inwardly with rage and humiliation.

"He's all that and more," Rome replied sharply. "And my guess is that the check he finally sent you was for only one thousand dollars, not for the twelve hundred that he actually got."

"Of course. And I was lucky to even get that."

"When you saw him today, did you tell him you knew that he'd gotten twelve hundred dollars for your clock?"

"No, and I don't intend to." She suppressed her anger under the appearance of indifference.

Rome looked at her intently. "He's committed

fraud, Abby. Why should you let him get away with it? Don't you even want a little revenge?''

She breathed a sigh. "The only thing I want, or ever wanted, was to get my clock back. But that's impossible." Abby shook her head sadly. "That dealer in Concord told me he sold my clock three days after he got it. So the fact is that I'll never see it again. Nothing is going to change that." She lowered her head now to escape Rome's scrutinizing gaze. "Now you know the whole story, Rome, and I really don't want to talk or even think about it anymore," she said, reaching for her glass of iced tea. "What's done is done. Time to chalk it all up to experience and forget it."

"You're right, of course," Rome said. "I'll help you any way I can. You can count on it." He spoke with conviction and seemed to exude a quiet strength that Abby found reassuring.

Chapter Nine

"Abby, I need to stop back by the inn for a few minutes," Rome said, as they left Zeke's and were walking back to Abby's shop, where Rome had left his car. "Jacoby will be there by this time, and I have the detailed reports on the location areas he wanted set up for the first week of filming." He looped his arm through hers, urging her to quicken her steps. "It won't take me more than ten minutes. You don't mind do you?"

" 'Course not," she answered, taking long strides to match his. "But who's Jacoby?"

"Clifford Jacoby—he's the director for *A Different Drummer*. Considered one of the best, too."

"Do you know him, then?" she asked.

"That I do." Rome's voice mirrored enthusiasm. "I worked with him on a movie two years ago. He's a stickler for set details, but he's patient, and that makes him a nice guy to work with."

"Sounds interesting. Is he oldish or youngish?"

Rome eyed her wryly. "He's fortyish and I'm relatively sure he's married with a couple of kids. Besides, I'm the only guy connected with this movie that you're supposed to find *interesting*." He hugged her arm possessively. "I'm your main man!" he declared emphatically.

Abby glanced up at him and smiled. "Are you saying you're my big squeeze?"

"That too," he said, laughing and giving her a broad wink. "And don't you forget it."

"I'll try my best not to," she said, laughing back at him.

Abby sat down on the camelback sofa in the front parlor of the Lindenwood Inn to wait while Rome located Clifford Jacoby. She always enjoyed being inside the interesting and attractive inn. While not as old as Hampton House, it had much of the same character and ambience. It was, however, a much larger and more elaborate structure. The interior focused around an imposing center hallway on the first floor. The rooms off the hallway were unusually large, and the second and third floors boasted ten bedrooms, each with its own fireplace and bath. The exterior was embellished with turrets, domes, and dark shutters, while throughout the inn, furniture, marble mantels, and ornate doorstops added to its elegance.

In a very short time Rome returned, bringing Cliff with him. "When Rome told me the owner of Hampton House was waiting downstairs, I insisted on coming down to meet you," the director said, shaking Abby's hand warmly. "I wanted to tell you in person how much we're all looking forward to making our movie in that wonderful, historic house of yours. Thank you for allowing us that privilege.'' His deep voice was unhurried and somehow soothing.

Abby wondered if Rome had told him she'd had qualms about them using her house and if that was the reason he was making an effort to be so cordial. Whatever the reason, she liked his unpretentious, friendly manner. There was no doubt in her mind that if she were an actress she'd surely welcome him as her director. ''I'm glad you chose Hampton House,'' Abby said graciously. ''I'm sure you know that this entire business of having a movie made right here in our town is terrifically exciting to all of us.''

''Good. Local enthusiasm is welcome and needed if we're to have a one hundred percent successful film.'' He smiled at her as his acorn-brown eyes studied her with detached interest from under dark, heavy brows. ''I understand from Rome that you are in the antique business, and that your shop is located near the town square.''

Abby nodded. ''Rome found the location for me and it's working out nicely.''

''Abby's always had her shop in her house, Cliff,'' Rome jumped into the conversation to explain. ''Brent Ritchey and I helped her set up shop downtown just for the duration of the filming. She'll be moving her business back to Hampton House when the movie is finished, won't you Abby?''

"I will, of course—but not immediately. I guess I haven't told you, but I've got some big plans I hope to carry out this fall at Hampton House." She looked at Rome, with eyes that glowed with a sheen of purpose. "With the money I'm getting from your studio, I'm going to have the carriage house converted into a splendid shop for Hampton House Antiques. You get your movie and I get the shop I've dreamed of. In my book, it doesn't get much better than that," she said gaily.

"And it doesn't get any better for a guy looking for some company than to find the three of you right here."

Surprised to hear someone addressing them, they all three turned around to see Drew watching them from the doorway. "In that case, come join us," Cliff said genially. "Abby was just telling us about some future plans she has for her antique shop."

"Abby has a great little business going all right," Drew commented, immediately coming over to join them. "I saw that this afternoon when I tracked her down so she and I could renew our old friendship." He flashed her a smile. "We shared some good times here in the White Mountains, didn't we, Pigeon?"

Abby stiffened and pressed her lips tensely together, making no effort to respond. Rome instantly placed his arm around her shoulders, pressing her to his side. "Abby met Drew when he was here with a summer theater troupe about four or five years ago," Rome quickly explained to Cliff. "Rather an odd coincidence that now he's back in New Hampshire for this film, wouldn't you say? Just proves it's a small world after all." He paused and hugged Abby's shoulder. "And now, Cliff, you and Drew may want to discuss Monday's shoot while Abby and I run along." As Rome was saying this he was backing away and drawing Abby with him. They made their escape very quickly.

As soon as they were out of earshot, Abby glanced at him and said, "That was a masterful manuever, even for a Scotsman."

"Aye, it was that," Rome agreed without a shred of modesty.

By the first of the following week the production staff, the camera crews, the stars and feature players, in fact every person connected with the making of *A Different Drummer*, had arrived in Lindenwood. The town was aglow with excitement, and overnight it was full of the hubbub of activity. Abby could not escape having a small part in it. And though she had once declared that she took no particular interest in movies or movie stars, she, like every other citizen of Lindenwood, was fascinated from day one with everything that was taking place.

Abby learned from Rome that Jacoby's schedule for the first weeks of filming was to shoot the majority of the outdoor scenes. He wanted to complete this portion of the movie during the mild summer weather, with its abundance of blooming flowers and green grassy fields for background.

There were to be numerous scenes around the courthouse and public buildings. Another place of importance in the film was to be the white steepled church with its two hundred–year-old cemetery. "It is that old picturesque church and your house that made us choose Lindenwood for the location for *A Different Drummer*," Rome had told Abby that day when he first came to Hampton House. Now he told her that when Jacoby got his first glimpse of the church he said it looked as if it came straight out of a Currier & Ives picture. In fact, he was so taken with it that not only was it to be used in the summer wedding sequence which would be filmed in these first few weeks, but he wanted the writers to alter another major scene between Lee Greenway and Stephanie Marlowe so it could be filmed in the churchyard in late September, at the height of the glorious New England fall foliage.

Of course the news of a movie being filmed in Lindenwood drew in lots of sightseers from the other villages in the mountain area. This was a boon to the local businesses. Lots of folks wandered into Abby's shop, but they were mostly just lookers. That's to be expected in the antique business, however.

One particular morning, an interior decorator from up at Franconia came in intent on scouting for nineteenth-century wall hangings and decorative accessories for one of her clients. She carried a tape measure with her, taking measurements of various items, and making notes in a pocket-size notebook. She questioned Abby about a few things, but in the main she just browsed. When she left, she took Abby's phone number, saying she'd get back with her after consulting with her client.

An instant later, Kay Wheeler came dashing into the store. "You won't believe what happened to me," she cried. "I went to the town square early this morning. There were scads of people there—lots that you know. And this man, who is the movie director, I think. He was there. He kept pointing out certain folks, men, women, and even a couple of teenagers. He'd say, 'you there—the tall fellow with the glasses—that lady carrying a big white purse—and that boy in jeans and a T-shirt.' It was a *cattle call,* they said. Then all of a sudden this director wagged his finger at me. 'You in the blue striped vest—step over here,' he yelled. It was me! He picked me," Kay's voice spiraled in elation.

"Slow down! You're talking a mile a minute and I can't follow you." Abby was completely nonplussed by what Kay was saying. "What in heaven's name is a cattle call?"

"That's showbiz talk. It's the way they go about hiring extras for crowd scenes and walk-ons in the movies," Kay said glibly, looking just a tad smug at being so knowledgeable. "And wait until you hear what I got to do. I was actually just this far from

Stephanie Marlowe.'' Kay held up both hands to indicate about twelve inches. ''I was standing directly
behind her in the courthouse. I'm certain you'll catch
sight of most of me. At least my head and shoulders.
Boy am I glad I wore this striped vest. I think that
director picked me because he noticed my bright blue
vest. At any rate, I'm actually going to be seen in the
movie. Isn't that the living end?'' She crossed her
arms, hugging herself in her excitement.

''Sounds terrific. I can't wait to hear what Joe says
when he hears his wife is appearing in a major
movie.'' Abby grinned. ''He's going to be the husband
of a local celebrity. And who knows? They might even
premier the movie here in Lindenwood.''

''Wow! That would be out of this world. Do you
really think there's a chance they'd do that?''

''I have no idea what they might do. But it's possible that they'd do it in New Hampshire at least.
We'll just have to wait and see.''

''You know, Abby, seeing as how they're using
your house for this movie, you really should appear in
at least one scene somewhere,'' Kay said, wagging her
index finger in Abby face. ''So here's exactly what
you must do. Come with me to the next cattle call. I
heard somebody say this morning that there will be
another one next week some time when they get ready
to film a wedding scene at St. Paul's Church. It would
be great fun to be in that. We'd could be all dressed
up and look pretty. I'd love that, wouldn't you?''

Abby hunched her shoulders, making a wry face.

"I'm afraid I'd just feel awkward and sort of foolish."

"No you wouldn't. I bet a bunch of our friends will be dying to be picked and get their faces on camera. Believe me, they'll turn out for this, so you'd better too," she told Abby emphatically. "Promise me you'll think about it."

"Okay, I'll think about it," she said halfheartedly.

Kay looked at her watch. "I've got to run. It's ten after twelve and Joe said he'd be home for lunch at twelve-thirty. I promised to have egg salad sandwiches and I haven't even boiled the eggs yet." She rushed off like a blue streak.

Abby stood in the center of the shop, absently rubbing her finger back and forth across her chin and staring thoughtfully into space. The vision of that sublime dress that she'd bought in Boston when she was there last spring for the international antique auction sale was parading through her mind. It was this incredible shade of azure, and when she'd tried it on it fit her to perfection, and the style and color were the the most becoming of any dress she'd ever seen. So, though the price was a bit more than she was used to paying, still she felt she'd die if she didn't buy it.

Abby sighed as she recalled all of this, and then she gave a gleeful little chuckle. Kay was absolutely right. *A Different Drummer* was being made in her house and therefore she not only ought to be in a scene, but she deserved to be. And after all, she did have the perfect dress to appear in at a New England summer wedding.

Chapter Ten

Abby kept her plans to attend the next cattle call a secret from Rome. She did this not only because she felt somewhat self-conscious about doing it, but also because she didn't want him making a big deal out of it. As it turned out, there was no problem about getting picked as an extra. Jacoby dismissed all children under sixteen years of age and anyone with allergies to flower pollen. ''We will have the church banked with flowers and we can't have a sneeze or a cough spoiling the wedding ceremony, now can we?'' he said, smiling. ''So everyone else be at the church at one o'clock tomorrow afternoon. Men in coats and ties, women in dresses. You're guests at a wedding, so look your best.'' He shooed them away then with a quick wave, and turned his attention to this day's shoot.

The following afternoon, Abby and Kay arrived at the church ten minutes ahead of time. There was a lot of activity going on. The director and his staff, plus numerous cameramen, were there talking together or shifting equipment from one area of the church to another. And numerous actors and actresses in costume and makeup hovered about in preparation for the filming of the wedding scene.

As the rest of the extras joined Abby and Kay, they were all herded down the aisle and directed into the various pews by two of the director's assistants. Their arrangement seemed to be determined by the color of their clothes, the height of their heads when seated, and the proper interspersing of men among the women. Once this seating was arranged, Jacoby studied the assemblage for several minutes, shifted a few people, and moved both Abby and Kay into seats on the center aisle.

"Now you are the wedding guests, and a wedding is a joyous occasion. So I want you all to act pleased to be here to witness this beautiful ceremony," Jacoby instructed them. "You will hear the wedding march, then the flower girls will start the procession down the center aisle. As the wedding party passes by the row where you're sitting, glance at them with admiring interest. Your part is as simple as that," he assured them with a bland smile.

As it turned out, they shot the scene three times before Cliff was totally satisfied. "That's a take!" he said, sounding well pleased. "And thank you one and all," he added as he immediately cleared the church of all the extras with a gesture of dismissal.

As Abby filed down the aisle after Kay and the others, she caught sight of Brent. He signaled her with his outstretched hand. "Wait a minute," he mouthed the words to her.

She stepped back into one of the rows and stood there until he could work his way across to her. "I'm hoping your camera caught me at my best angle," she joked, laughing.

"Couldn't miss. You look good from every angle." He teased her with a rakish glance. "And I can't wait to tell the Scotsman that he missed your movie debut."

"Where is Rome anyway? I thought sure he'd be here."

"I don't think he had any idea you were going to do this, Abby. I'm sure he'd have been here if he had," Brent said, rubbing his hand back and forth across his forehead absently. "He said something about having to drive over to some import store on route sixteen. Something to do with the Scottish Games that are coming up around here in a few weeks." He frowned. "Didn't make very much sense to me. Do you know what he was talking about?"

"Sure do. It's the annual festival of the New Hampshire Highland Games. A big gathering of the Scottish clans—so it figures that Rome would really be into that. Maybe he's getting a kilt and plans to dance the Highland Fling," she quipped with a chortle.

"That I've got to see," Brent declared emphatically.

"Me too!" Abby agreed, an impish smile making her eyes twinkle.

"Look, I've got to go, 'cause Jacoby wants to film another couple of scenes with Stephanie Marlowe in the wedding dress. But I do have something I want to talk to you about. Can I call you later?"

"I guess so—sure." She narrowed her eyes at him curiously.

"Good. I'll ring you at home when I'm through here. Probably be six or so," he said, turning and heading back to the area where he'd come from.

Puzzled, Abby stared after him. What was on his mind, she wondered? Brent was Rome's friend, and though the three of them had been together quite a lot, and he had pitched in to help Rome get her antiques moved into her new shop for her, still she hadn't spoken with him all that much. She was surprised that he'd made a point of wanting to talk to her about something. She couldn't imagine what it could possibly be. She shrugged, thinking it probably was nothing much. She pushed her speculations from her mind and marched hurriedly up the aisle.

Outside the church, the afternoon ran slowly, heavy like honey, sweet and golden and not oppressive. The air was fragrant with honeysuckle and spicy with the smell of cedar. Abby quickly decided that by the time she could get home and change her clothes it would be far too late to even consider going back downtown to her shop. Besides, surely as a first-time movie extra she rated the rest of the afternoon off. Too, she still had a number of personal things she wanted to secret away in her private bedroom wing area of the house. The movie company was already in its fourth week of filming. It was reasonable to expect that they would be ready to start the inside scenes in Hampton House within another week. In fact, that could be what Brent had wanted to speak to her about. He was the head cameraman. He'd know exactly when they were to move their equipment in and begin.

Having convinced herself that she'd best use what time remained today to collect her special little treasures that were scattered around her house and stow them out of view, she donned a comfortable pair of cutoff, stone-washed jeans and her oldest and softest cotton knit tennis shirt. Left over from her college days, this once bright canary yellow shirt had survived countless washings and days of being line-dried in the sun, until now it was scarcely yellow at all. In fact, one of those small cartons of whipped margarine had more color than it did. She tucked her shirttail into the waistband of her jeans with a satisfied sigh. From her elegant silk dress to this, she'd gone from the sublime to the scruffy—it just proved she had the wardrobe to fit every occasion. She suppressed a contented giggle and sashayed out of her bedroom.

As she walked through the other rooms gathering up the things she wanted, a breeze lifted the lace curtains, dallied a moment, and vanished in the stillness of the house.

Abby welcomed the quiet; it was peaceful and filled her with a pleasant feeling of nostalgia. She loved every inch of this two-hundred-year-old house. Not only because it now belonged solely to her, but because it reflected the lives of the generations of Hamptons that came before her. Like the characters in the movie Allied was filming here, each of those Hampton men and women had heard a different drummer, and each had stepped to the music that he or she could hear.

It was close to six-thirty that evening when Brent telephoned. ''We just finished filming at the church, and I bet I'm calling right in the middle of your supper,'' he said, a note of apology in his voice.

''No, I haven't gotten around to thinking about eating yet. Actually, when the phone rang I was hoping it was you. I'm eager to find out what you wanted to talk to me about.''

''I'm not sure I should bother you with this, Abby.'' There was a note of hesitancy in his words. ''But I figured you should know, and I doubted that Rome would worry you with it.''

''Boy, now you're making me curious as a Siamese kitten. So tell me, for Pete's sake. What is it?''

''It's this fellow, Drew Daniels. He's some big talker. He's sounding off all over the set. Mostly, though, he corners Rome every chance he gets wanting to talk to him about you. Today, with Rome gone, he zeroed in on me.''

''Drew is so full of himself and such an aggravating bore. Try to ignore him, Brent. That's what I'm doing.''

''I'm going to do my best to avoid him from here on out. But today I couldn't get away from him. He's really hung up on you, you know, and he's plenty nosy. He pestered me with a bunch of stupid questions and then just flat-out asked me if I thought things were serious between you and Rome.''

''He has more brass than brains,'' Abby said, not attempting to hide her annoyance. ''I hope you told him to knock it off and mind his own business.''

''Well I didn't use those exact words.'' Brent chuckled. ''I simply told him honestly that I hadn't given the subject a single thought, seeing as how it was stricly a matter between the Scotsman and his lady.''

''Well put. That should have put Drew in his place.'' Abby's voice brightened. ''Did it?''

''He didn't ask me any more questions at least.''

''Good. That's progress. Now with luck he'll let up on both Rome and you.''

''Are you okay with this, Abby? I mean, you're not upset or worried about it?''

''Oh, a little, of course. But I needed to know what Drew is saying—and thanks for clueing me in. . . .''

Abby hung up then, but she didn't immediately move away from the phone. She sat there, a troubled frown marking her face. Brent had felt that it was important for her to know that Drew had been talking about her to Rome. He'd also implied that Rome was not going to worry her by mentioning it to her himself. But why not? What reasons would Rome have for not wishing to discuss it with her? She was beginning to feel extremely uneasy. If Drew had nerve enough to ask Brent the questions that he did, then he was crass enough to try to sound out Rome about his personal feelings. Abby flinched at the thought of Rome's reaction to such an invasion of his privacy.

Abby's stomach felt jumpy, and her head, which had started to thud when she was on the phone with Brent, was really throbbing now. She got slowly to her feet and walked without haste but with purpose into the kitchen. Drew had brought havoc to her life once before, but there was no way under heaven she was going to let him do it again.

She fixed herself a glass of instant iced tea, and started drinking it as she went about getting her supper. Removing a package of crab cakes from the freezer, she put two in the microwave and then tossed leaf lettuce, tomato, cucumber, and two sliced radishes for a salad, generously coating the ingredients with French dressing. Just the sight of food brightened her outlook, and the thought that she could finish off her meal with a big scoop of her favorite pistachio nut ice cream made her spirits soar.

She set a place at her kitchen table and was about to flip on the radio to a round-the-clock music station when she heard two long and two short blasts of a car horn, which was Rome announcing his arrival in her driveway. The sounds seemed unusually close, as if he'd driven clear up the driveway to the carriage house. This proved to be true, for in less than a minute Abby heard footsteps on the breezeway. The next instant Rome was banging on her kitchen door. She quickly unlocked the back door and stepped back to let him in.

"Hi, you're just in time for dinner, that is if you'll settle for crab cakes."

"No thanks. I didn't eat lunch until late, because the owner of the import shop where I went to pick up the things I'd ordered insisted I had to eat a meal at this Scottish Lion Restaurant that features a Scottish menu. It was great all right, only trouble is, it's hearty food and mighty filling. I'm not up to eating anything more today, that's for sure."

"Sounds like a red-letter day for a Scotsman like you," Abby said, a faint glint of humor lighting her eyes.

"Aye, it was that." His voice echoed his contented expression. "And I brought you some souvenirs of Scotland." He held up the colorful plaid shopping bag that he'd carried in.

Abby's expression was one of surprise and delight. "You're one great guy, Rome. I just love getting a present." She held out an eager hand, smiling up at him. "What is it? Let me see."

"Nothing to get excited about. I just brought you a little touch of Scotland. Besides, the shop owner gave me the box of shortbread. Said it would go with what I'd bought," Rome said with a sheepish grin as he handed the plaid shopping bag to her.

"I'm crazy about shortbread; it's so good it's sinful." Abby took the package of butter-rich cookies from the top of the bag. Then she reached in and pulled out two square tin boxes. "Oho, perfect—imported teas to go with the shortbread," she exclaimed, her lilting voice going up like notes on a music scale. "And there's even more." She set the bag on the table because she needed two hands to lift out the bulky square box in the bottom of the sack. "What's in this big, interesting-shaped box?"

"Open it and find out," Rome quipped.

The box was carefully packed with lots of shredded paper and the contents wrapped in tissue. Abby unwrapped each item cautiously to discover a teapot and four cups in the distinctive Buchan Thistleware pottery. "I love it," she cried. "We'll simply have to initiate my Scottish tea set together this very evening. I know you claim you're not hungry, but at least you can drink tea and eat one very small cookie."

A wide grin glowed across Rome's face and Abby

could tell that it had made him happy to see how pleased she was with what he'd brought her. She couldn't resist reaching up, putting her arms around his neck, and giving him a quick, light kiss.

"Why did I rate that?" he asked, his eyes caressing her upturned face.

She looked up at him, her eyes soft and dreamy. "I—I can't tell you exactly," she said, a note of hesitation in her voice. "I'll just say I think it has something to do with you being Scottish." She gave a brief little laugh, passing it off as a playful joke.

She turned away then and immediately got busy taking her dinner out of the microwave. There was no way she could explain to Rome what she now realized. And that was that she was utterly vulnerable to him because the sound of his voice and the shape of his eyes, the edge of his laughter, and the look of his mouth and hands had all become charged with meaning for her. The plain and simple truth was that she was in love with him, and she didn't know what she should, or even could, do about it.

Chapter Eleven

"Maybe you didn't notice, Abby, but when I came tonight I drove all the way to the back and parked in front of the carriage house. I've been waiting for you to ask me why I did this."

The two of them were sitting at the kitchen table drinking the tea Rome had brought and nibbling on the Scottish shortbread. Abby looked at Rome over the edge of her cup. "I realized where you'd left your car when you came to the kitchen door," she said, not showing any particular interest.

"Well, aren't you curious as to why I did that when I've never done it before?"

"Not particularly." She paused long enough to reach for another square of shortbread. "I know driving to the back and coming in at the back of the house takes less time and fewer steps. I suppose that could have been your reason, especially since you were carrying in that shopping bag full of nice presents for me." Abby's mood was buoyant, and it showed in her voice and shone in her eyes.

"That had nothing to do with it," he grumbled, pretending to be a little insulted by her statement. "I had a far better motive that that. One that concerns something I'd like to do if it would be of any help or interest to you.''

''I can hardly tell you that until I know what it is. So will you please stop beating around the bush and just tell me right out what you're talking about?'' She gave him a cajoling smile. ''I'm dying to know, really.''

''I thought you'd never ask.'' A faintly eager look flashed in Rome's eyes. ''You see, ever since you mentioned that you wanted to turn the carriage house into your antique shop, I've been wanting to see it and hear about your plans. If you'd like me to, I could make some sketches using your ideas as to how you want the interior arranged. Also, I'd sort of like to help you design the outside entrance and the front of the shop, just to give you a few ideas.'' He paused and held his raised hand out toward her like a policeman halting traffic. ''Mind you, this is just something I'd like to try my hand at for fun. I have a couple of ideas, but they may not appeal to you at all, and you can toss 'em out. I won't mind a bit. I mean it!''

Abby stared at him, her eyes wide as saucers. Once again she was totally surprised by this unpredictable man. ''Rome, you're incredible. I'd be tickled to death to have any help you'd give me. You're a set designer. You know how to put my dreams into a form so that I can visualize them. Nothing could be more welcome to me than that.'' Her voice vibrated with her enthusiasm. "I want to do this so much, and if you'll help me with the plans, I'll owe you big."

"Okay then, I'll collect a favor from you later on, providing I come up with a shop design that fits your dream, that is." Rome's grin edged into a caressing smile, his eyes travelling her face appreciatively.

Warmth sparked across the space between them, an arc of almost visible light. Abby swallowed, trying to regain her composure, for she'd never known a man who could affect her this way, a man whose gaze was like an intimate touch.

"Come on," she said, jumping up from the kitchen table. "Let's go look at the carriage house right now so you can get started."

Later, after Rome had left, Abby found herself humming happily as she placed her supper dishes in the dishwasher and set the kitchen in order. Still singing softly under her breath, she went upstairs to get ready for bed. It had been a full and rather exciting day, what with taking part in a movie shoot, and then having Rome show up bringing her presents.

Thinking about the evening, she realized Rome hadn't told her the reason he'd taken the day off to visit a Scottish import shop. She was a bit curious about this, wondering what it was he'd ordered for himself. She'd heard that every year at the Highland Games a trophy was awarded for the best arrayed gentleman in Highland dress. She knew too that spectators as well as clansmen were encouraged to wear the traditional dress of Scotland in its less military form. She wouldn't put it past Rome to do just that. He'd be a striking and handsome figure, she had no doubt of that. At any rate she'd know in a few weeks if Rome had bought himself a kilt, a balmoral cap, knee stockings, and those gillie brogue shoes, because the New Hampshire Highland Games were scheduled for a weekend in the middle of September.

Abby's happiness faded as this date occurred to her, for mid September was just a month away. By that time the filming of *A Different Drummer* would be completed. This meant that following the Scottish games, Rome would be returning to the West Coast with the others. Everything would be over—finished. The time she and Rome had shared together would come to an end, and so would their relationship. She'd do well to face that fact right now and start preparing herself for it.

There was a pensive shimmer now in the shadow of her eyes. She sat down on the side of her bed, her face clouded with disquieting thoughts. What she and Rome were having was a light, brief romance, one without promises and without commitments. Rome was a free spirit, and Abby felt that he wasn't looking for a serious or lasting relationship. Certainly he hadn't intended for her to fall in love with him, and she must never let him discover that she had.

For a few moments she sat there, moving her head

hopelessly from side to side, caught up in the squirrel cage of her painful thoughts while tears webbed her thick lashes like silver threads.

Abby had no idea how long she had sat there or what time it was, but with the sudden ringing of the telephone she was jarred into awareness that the hour was extremely late for anyone to be calling her for a casual chat.

"Listen, I bet you're in bed, but I hope you weren't asleep," Rome announced, the instant that Abby answered her phone.

"No, not yet. I'm just getting ready for bed."

"I'm glad I didn't wake you. I just felt it was important to tell you about what happened tonight."

There was a note of excitement in Rome's voice that intrigued Abby. "What happened? Where and to whom?"

"First, Jacoby suddenly called for a night shoot. Seems the moon was out and just in the right position to film a scene in the cemetery next to the church. They wrapped up the shoot about eleven o'clock I guess, because Jacoby, Drew, and Lee Greenway were just going up to their rooms when I got back to the inn from your house. Drew latched onto me, and insisted on coming to my room to talk. I tried, but I couldn't get away from him."

Abby groaned. "Drew is totally incorrigible. Did Brent tell you that Drew waylaid him this afternoon when they filmed the wedding scene?"

"I'm not surprised."

"Brent told him off. Suggested he mind his own business. I hope you'll ignore all the outlandish things Drew says as well. Because short of murder, I don't know what can be done to shut him up." Anger colored her words.

"No—wait. This time it was okay. I think Drew and I came to an understanding. That's why I called you. I wanted to tell you about it before tomorrow, because I have a feeling that Drew may try to see you in the morning. And if he does, you listen to him. He could possibly help you with something you want."

"That'll be the day!" she said derisively.

"I'm serious, Abby. Just let me tell you what Drew was so anxious to talk to me about."

"I can't believe he could say anything you wanted to hear." Abby's voice had a caustic edge.

"You may be surprised," Rome countered calmly.

Abby heaved a verbal sigh. "Rome, at this point, nothing Drew says or does could surprise me."

"Well, the bargain I made with him will. You see, he wants me to do something for him, so I asked him to do something in return."

Abby was aghast at hearing this. "Are you out of your mind? You don't bargain with someone like Drew. He can't be trusted to do anything he promises. He'll just get what he wants from you and welch out of his end of the deal."

"Not this time, he won't." Rome's voice had a confident ring. ''You see, I've got the upper hand,'' he chuckled. ''Or rather *you* do, Abby.''

''I do!'' she exclaimed in total amazement. ''What on earth are you really talking about? Will you please explain this to me in words of one syllable so I can understand what I've got to do with this thing that's going on between you and Drew?''

''All right, it's like this. It appears that when they finished the night shoot at the cemetery, Jacoby announced that starting the first of next week they'd be filming at Hampton House. Now while Drew has been nervous before about what you might tell the others about him, he's become as jumpy as a kangaroo on a trampoline at this point.''

''But why?''

''Because he figures that now that they'll all be in your house, day after day for three or four weeks, you'll have lots of opportunities to let everybody know what a sorry sort he is.''

''I've no intention of telling them about him.''

''But he doesn't know you won't. That's why you've got the upper hand, and also why I made this bargain with him. I said I'd use any influence I might have with you to convince you to keep silent, but he'd have to first get us some kind of a lead as to who bought your clock and how we could contact them. I explained to him that the important thing to you was getting your clock back. I also mentioned that you knew that he'd actually been paid twelve hundred dollars for the clock, not just one thousand.'' Rome paused, making a quick clicking sound with his tongue and teeth. ''I wish you could have seen Drew's expression when I told him that.''

''Tell me. Just how did he look?''

Rome laughed. ''All the color drained out of his pretty boy face and he seemed to shrivel up like a dry sponge.''

''You almost make me feel sorry for him.''

''Well don't. He deserves to suffer a little bit for what he did to you. Don't you dare let him off the hook until he comes up with a real lead for us.'' Rome's voice had a ring of uncompromising finality. They talked for only a few seconds more, then Rome said he'd better hang up and let her get some sleep.

As it turned out, she did go promptly to bed, but she had a restless night. She slept badly, a myriad of thoughts moving around in her head. So much time had elapsed. What possible chance would Drew, or anyone else, have of tracking down the whereabouts of the clock by now? In four years it could have been sold a number of times. What if another dealer had purchased it first? He might have sold it to a decorator, who then sold it to a client. The possibilities were endless. Abby tossed fitfully, halfway between waking and sleeping. How hopeless the search could be—like looking for a needle in a haystack. That's what her grandmother would say. . . . She moaned as she drifted in and out of confusing dreams. She awoke the following morning with tousled hair, dark-shadowed eyes, and traces of fatigue marking her face.

This mid-August weekend there was a music festival and craft fair being held in the town square. Numerous country western singers and rock groups performed through the day and evening, and a state-of-the-art sound system made it possible for Abby to hear the music in her shop almost as clearly as if she'd been standing with all the spectators in the square.

Abby had her shop open, but it was a quiet morning for her. Most everybody was milling through the craft booths shopping for handmade quilts, pottery, wood carvings, and handcrafted jewelry. Antiques are not the first priority with shoppers when a craft fair and open-air music festival take over the center of town.

Shortly after noon, Rome called and asked if he could come by the shop and pick up her house key from her. "Jacoby wants to take Stephanie and Lee through the house, give them a preview of everything before they start the actual shooting on Monday," he told her. "I'll be there in about fifteen minutes."

Abby hung up, but before she even had her hand off the receiver, the phone rang again.

"Abby, it's Drew. I'm calling you from Concord. I'm here at the antique shop where I sold your clock. I've just been talking to the dealer, Mott Collins."

He spoke in a quick rush of words and Abby got the idea that he wanted to get everything said in a hurry and without letting her interrupt.

"I expect Rome told you we'd had a little talk. He suggested that I try to get some information about the whereabouts of your clock." He paused just long enough to take a breath. "So I got hold of a car and drove down here this morning."

Abby's head was reeling from the surprise of learning that Drew was calling from Concord. He certainly hadn't wasted any time in finding some transportation and driving the eighty or so miles from Lindenwood to New Hampshire's capital. Rome wasn't kidding when he said she had the upper hand with Drew in the bargain he'd made with him. Realizing that Drew was waiting for her to make some comment, she said, "I appreciate your efforts. That's good of you."

"Well, I called because Mott Collins here needs you to give him some information so he can identify the clock to check his records. See what, if any, knowledge he can scrape up as to the person who bought it from him and how long ago it was. Here, I'll put Mr. Collins on the phone."

"Would you describe your clock for me please, miss," the dealer said, "I have a slight recollection of it I believe, but I've handled a number of decorative antique clocks and I'll need some details to help me pinpoint the one you're seeking." His deep-timbreed voice was courteous and businesslike. She wondered if he was the same man she'd talked to four years ago when she went down to Concord to arrange to make installment payments to redeem her clock. She had become so upset learning that Drew had lied to her and that her clock was gone, that she'd fled from the store without even asking the man his name. She flinched at the memory of that sad day.

"Yes, of course," she muttered hastily. "It's a porcelain table clock with the figure of a shepherd boy on the top. It was made in Austria. It bears the mark of the china maker, and from that I determined it was made between 1900 and 1910 in Vienna." Abby hesitated, thinking what else she might be able to tell him. "Oh yes, and about the decoration. It's done in shades of rose and green, with touches of yellow, some amber, and of course there is gold gilding on the base of the clock."

"I can tell you're very attached to this clock."

"I certainly am. You see, it belonged to my grandmother. It's a real family heirloom and one I never intended to part with. That is why I would give anything to be able to buy it back." She was getting emotional and her voice was shakier than she would have liked.

"Well, you've given me a good picture of your grandmother's clock, and I do have a vague recollection of my transaction with your friend, Mr. Daniels," Mott Collins said in a gentle tone that Abby felt had a note of compassion in it. "I'll tell you what. Give

me your name and address and phone number. I'll
check my records and get back to you.'' He hesitated,
clearing his throat. ''I have to warn you, however, that
unless I discover that I sold your clock to one of my
regular customers, there's little or no chance of locat-
ing it. You must understand that. After all, we're talking about something that took place four years ago.''

''Yes, I realize that, and I understand that my
chances are slim. But I do appreciate your taking the
time and effort to try to help me. Thank you.''

Abby gave him her name then and repeated her address and phone number slowly to allow him time to
write it down. Then she said good-bye and hung up
the phone without speaking again to Drew.

Chapter Twelve

Abby had a customer when Rome came in the shop to pick up the key to her house, so she didn't have an opportunity to tell him about Drew having called her from Concord. It actually didn't matter, because Jacoby and the others were waiting for Rome in the car and he couldn't have stopped to talk anyway.

A couple of hours later, Rome called to say that the others had finished at her house and were leaving, but he was going to stay on to work on plans for the carriage house. He'd keep busy and wait for her to come home. Liking the idea that he wished to wait there for her, she returned to work with a genial smile on her face.

Through the remainder of the afternoon only three more customers came in. She did make one sale, however, an ornate Victorian table made of rosewood and with a marble top. It was an exceptional piece and in good condition. Even though it was Abby's only sale for the day, it was a highly satisfactory one. In fact, she was so pleased that since it was a quarter until five, she placed the CLOSED sign in the front window and headed for home.

Her mood was now much changed from when she'd woken up this morning. She had to admit that it wasn't all due to her successful sale. Some of it was because Rome was waiting for her to come home—this plus the knowledge that he had wanted to get involved in her plans for remodeling the carriage house. To do all this must mean that he cared about her to some degree. A sparkle entered her eyes and a smile sprang to her lips. "Faint heart ne'er won fair lady," she said aloud. And faint heart never won a Scotsman either, she told herself, paraphrasing that old adage. Then she burst out laughing, because the one thing that had always been said about the Hampton women was that they were a stouthearted, determined lot.

Abby parked her car beside Rome's at the back of her drive. The carriage house doors were flung wide open, and Abby came inside to find Rome sitting Indian fashion in the center of the barnlike structure, a sketch pad on his lap.

"How on earth are you able to do that," she asked, walking leisurely toward him.

"Do what?" he said, angling his head up, his observing eyes admiring her shapely legs and the graceful way she carried herself as she moved to the center of the large room.

"Fold up those long, masculine legs of yours and sit cross-legged on the ground like a tribal chief."

"I'm just limber, I guess." He laughed.

She came up behind him. "I want to see what good

ideas you've come up with,'' she said, placing her hands on his shoulders and leaning over to view his drawing pad. ''Umm—mm, looks interesting, but you're going to have to explain what all those indentations, X's, and boxlike marks signify.'' She leaned down close to him as she pointed out the areas on his drawing, and as she did so her cheek brushed against the side of his face. This late in the day, a rough stubble had begun to edge Rome's cheek, and for some reason this made the touch of his face to hers as intimate as a caress. Abby experienced a feathery current of feeling racing through her. Instantly she pulled her head away, relieved that Rome didn't seem to have even noticed what she'd done.

''These bracket kind of marks indicate where I thought you might want windows installed.'' Rome pointed this out to her using the eraser end of his pencil. ''These would be regular double windows mainly, however, I thought possibly you'd like a large bay window here at the back. Depends on how much natural light you think you'd like.''

''That's something I hadn't thought about. This large an area will need a few windows, not only to let in light, but to give it the right look and make it fit in with the house.''

''Exactly. That's why at the front I picture a slightly modified version of the Federal Period door and styled windows that you have on the front of Hampton House.''

"Oh, I agree. That's exactly the look I want." Her voice spiraled. In her enthusiasm she squeezed Rome's shoulders without being conscious of doing it.

He turned his head and smiled up at her. "Of course that includes an elliptical fanlight over the entrance."

"Yes, a fanlight over the door is an absolute must. Inside too, I want the interior lighting to be in character. I want to use antique chandeliers." She hesitated, glancing around at the unfinished interior of the carriage house. "Of course this place is really not much more than a barn now," she said with a sigh. "But once they add insulation and put in finished interior walls and a finished ceiling, I can decide what lights will be the most effective and also be adequate to display a shop full of antiques to the very best advantage. That's what we're after here, right?"

Rome reached up and patted her left hand where it still rested on his shoulder. "Right as rain," he said, keeping his hand pressed warmly over hers. "I'd say you've thought this out pretty doggone well. I don't have much to add."

"Yes you do. I like your large bay window idea. I'd never have thought of that, and it's the perfect answer. I'll want glass shelves in that window so I can fill them with all colors of antique glassware—ruby, amber, amethyst, green, opal, yellow, and cobalt blue. Why, the sunlight coming through that bay window will reflect a whole rainbow of colors. It will be sensational!" Abby's delight in Rome's idea escalated as she talked about it. In her exuberance she lifted her hands off Rome's shoulders and started walking to the far end of the carriage house. "Get up and come with me, Rome," she yelled back over her shoulder. "I need you to measure this wall and help me figure out just how wide and how deep a bay window we can have. And bring your pencil so I can make some marks on the wood." She had reached the back wall now and was scrutinizing it thoughtfully.

Rome came up to stand behind her, folding his arms around her and resting his chin on her head. "You know, Abby, I'm really glad I came up with something that you're so enthusiastic about."

She stood motionless, enjoying feeling his arms around her waist and having his tall body warming the length of her back. "It's the ideal addition, and exactly what my shop needs. And you're the brilliant set designer that came up with it for me."

"Flattery like that will get you anything you ask for," he said, turning her around to face him, his gaze making a slow search of her face, a glimmer of longing in his eyes. He framed her upturned face in his hands, his thumb stroking the slender curve of her throat. "But before you start thinking about cutting out a big chunk of this back wall, you need to hire a remodeling contractor. He'll show you a catalog of the varied styles of windows that are available. The two of you can then make a decision about the size of bay window that will be the most effective here. Don't you agree with me on that?'' he asked, as his fingers began to gently trace the contours of her face.

"I—I guess so. Only I wanted to get your input.'' She could feel her skin tingling at his caressing touch, and the tremor of pleasure that was rippling through her made it difficult for her to make her voice sound normal.

"I can give it to you at that time.''

"But you'll be gone then. The movie will be finished and you'll be in California.''

"Maybe not,'' he said softly. "We'll have to wait and see what happens between now and then.'' His look was unreadable, and she hadn't the faintest conception of what she should make of his cryptic words.

As her eyes remained fastened on his, she saw his darken with passion. He circled his arms around her, pulling her tightly against him. She came willingly, savoring the fresh masculine smell of his skin and the soft motion of his lips on hers. He rained a shower of light kisses on her mouth followed by more intense questing ones. She stood perfectly still within his embrace, her pulse racing and her senses responding deliciously to his touch. There was no escape from the arms that held her and the mouth which had captured hers with a sensuality that drew an instant response from her.

When they finally drew apart, Abby looked at him wordlessly, conscious of the unsteady beat of her heart, and an inner trembling that had nothing to do with weakness—rather, it was evidence of the powerful effect of this Scotsman's kiss. . . .

Understandably, Abby and Rome had forgotten that the wide double doors to the carriage house were standing open, so it startled them both when a man's voice hailed them. "What are you two doing in this gloomy old barn? I saw your cars and I've been looking all over for you."

Rome spun around and took Abby's hand. Then they walked to the front to meet Drew, who stood with both hands planted on his hips staring in at them. "Abby's planning to convert this place into a permanent shop for her antiques. We're just looking around to figure out some of the possibilities."

"Yeah, Rome came up with a wonderful suggestion for a large window in the back wall—something to let daylight in and be decorative as well." She used an abundance of words as she struggled to regain her composure and act as if when Drew arrived she and Rome were doing nothing more exciting than inspecting the interior of the carriage house.

"You can use some light all right. Dark enough in there to house bats," Drew quipped.

"And it might have back in the 1800s," Abby countered with a shrug. "But it's going to house my antique business within the next six months or so," she stated confidently.

"So, now that you know why we're here, why don't you tell us who you came looking for—Abby or me?"

"Abby," Drew answered, turning his full attention to her. "I just got back in town, Abby, and I wanted to relay everything I learned from Mott Collins."

Rome shot Abby a questioning look. "Who's Mott Collins?"

"He's the man who owns the antique shop in Concord where Drew sold my clock. I didn't have a chance to tell you about it, but Drew drove down to Concord this morning. He telephoned me from the shop so I could answer some questions about my clock for this man."

Interest quickened on Rome's face. "That sounds a little bit encouraging, doesn't it?"

"Maybe. I don't know yet."

"What do you mean?"

"Well, he has to check and see if he has any record of who bought it from him. It was a pretty long time ago, and at first he didn't even seem to recall the clock. But after I described it, and reminded him of the time I came in and talked to him about it, he seemed to think he remembered it." She shrugged and turned her attention away from Rome to Drew. "He seemed like he was willing to try to help. Didn't you think so, Drew?" Abby looked inquiringly at the actor.

"That's what I came to tell you." Drew's expression stilled and grew serious. "He did want me to explain something to you. He said it was a matter of policy and that you being a dealer yourself would understand his position."

Abby's brow creased in a worried frown. ''What does my being an antique dealer have to do with it?''

''Well, he said that even if he does know who bought your clock, he can't tell you the person's name or allow you to contact him directly. However, what he will do is explain your situation, tell this person that you wish to talk to him about the possibility of buying your clock back, and he will give him your name. Then this guy can contact you if he chooses to. Collins said that was the best he would be able to do. From something he let slip when he was telling me all this, I got the idea that the person who he thinks bought it is a good customer of his, and evidently has bought a number of expensive imports from him. He referred to the fact that reputable dealers don't give out their customers' names, nor do they talk about what they may or may not have purchased.''

Abby's face fell. ''He's right. I can't argue with him on that. He figures I'm an emotional female that would go to absurd lengths to get her clock back. He's protecting his customer and himself this way, and I can't blame him.'' She heaved a disappointed sigh. ''My guess is that the chances of hearing from this person are slim.''

''Hey, slim is better than no chance at all,'' Rome said, putting a comforting arm around her shoulders. ''Look on the bright side. This Collins fellow at least does recall the buyer of your clock, and he is going to talk to him and tell him about you. That's a positive step.''

"And Abby, I want you to know I really tried to help. I know I owe it to you to do all I possibly can," Drew mumbled contritely.

"You can say that again," Rome's tone was caustic.

Abby held up a restraining hand. "I'd say we've all done what we could. So now we'll just have to wait and see what happens." There was a note of finality in her voice, and she made it perfectly clear that the discussion of the clock was over by walking away from the carriage house.

Chapter Thirteen

Steady and persistent, the rasping buzz of her alarm clock awakened Abby. With one hand, she groped for the clock and silenced it. Then she stretched both arms over her head and flexed her fingers before pushing aside the covers and sliding her slender legs over the side of the bed.

For the past two and a half weeks, ever since Allied started filming at Hampton House, this had been her new routine. She'd get up a bit earlier to make certain she would be showered, dressed, and out of the way before the cast and crew arrived. She'd leave in the morning before the day's filming started, and not return until they'd completed the shoot, which usually was by six in the evening.

Abby had made the necessary preparations to insure that her routine for these few weeks would work out well for her. She'd taken an electric coffee maker and a toaster oven down to the shop. She'd also brought down the little square refrigerator that she'd had at college, and she kept it well supplied with breakfast needs—fruit juices, instant breakfast drinks, and cream cheese and jelly for her bagels.

137

Since she'd had her antique shop downtown, she was already accustomed to closing up for an hour at noon and eating lunch at Zeke's, or one of the other restaurants that were located in the vicinity of the town square. And Rome, who'd made it his job to insure that she not be in any way inconvenienced by Allied's filming *A Different Drummer* in her home, insisted that she go out to dinner with him each night.

"I'll agree on one condition," she told him. "Since most days they'll finish at or before six o'clock, I'll cook dinner for you, or we'll get carryout and eat at my place. If the filming runs late, or Jacoby wants one of those night shoots you talk about, then you can take me out."

Rome concurred with her on this plan, and so the pattern for the final weeks of the filming had been established.

Things were slow at the shop that morning. Abby took advantage of the quiet to inventory a box of antique tiles. Recently at Lancaster, a New Hampshire town that was settled in 1764, an early-eighteenth-century house had been taken down, and the tiles from the numerous fireplaces in the house were salvaged for the antique market. Abby had been especially excited about these, as they originally came from Holland and were delft tiles in blue and white with a high glaze. The subjects of the designs included rural scenes, ships and sea monsters, one set depicting children at play, and a set of Aesop's fables tiles that dated back to 1760. She knew she would have numerous sales for these in the next few weeks, for the fall foliage tours always brought a number of antique shoppers.

Abby was busy arranging a display of the delft tiles when Kay Wheeler breezed gaily through the door. She immediately began asking Abby for all the latest news on all that was taking place at Hampton House. ''I want to hear every tiny little detail. What do they say to you? How do they all act? Is Stephanie Marlowe friendly or standoffish? And Lee Greenway, what's he like when you talk to him face-to-face? Tell me about everything, and please don't skip the juicy little bits,'' she pleaded eagerly.

Abby stopped what she was doing and looked at Kay in a kind of amused dismay. ''Really, Kay, how many times do I have to tell you that I really don't see or talk to the movie actors? I'm not at the house during the time they're working there.''

Kay looked as deflated as a burst balloon. ''Well, I don't see why you don't hang around at least some of the time. It is your house, you know. You have every right in the world to stay there and watch all that's going on. So why won't you?''

''I don't want to, that's why,'' Abby replied bluntly.

Kay stared at her friend, dumbfounded. ''I don't get you, Abby. Why, I can't imagine anything more exciting than watching Stephanie Marlowe and Lee Greenway in a great romantic scene. She's so gorgeous and he's—well, I could swoon over him. I think he's too exciting for words. Don't you?''

Abby pressed her lips together to keep from laughing. ''I think he's a pleasant, attractive man and an extremely fine actor. But he's also married, and I make it a practice not to swoon over thirty-five-year-old actors who have a wife and a couple of kids,'' Abby stated with a benign smile.

Kay made a face at her. ''Oh, you're such a realist, Abby Hampton. And if you weren't my best friend I'd cross you off as a lost cause. But as it is, I shall bide my time, because sure as fishes swim and birds fly, your swooning day is coming,'' she said, laughing. ''And sooner than you think.'' With this, Kay gave Abby a knowing wink and marched out the door.

Abby returned to the tiles and in a short time had them all attractively displayed near the front of the store. She glanced at the eight-day Seth Thomas mantel clock and saw that it was lunch time. She was just putting a sign in the front window CLOSED FOR LUNCH, BACK AT ONE O'CLOCK, and as she turned from the window her phone rang.

''Hampton House Antiques,'' Abby answered promptly.

''I'd like to speak to Abby Hampton if I may, please,'' a woman's gentle voice requested.

''This is she. How may I help you?'' Abby asked in her warm, cordial manner.

''My name is Gerda Halpern. The owner of Golden

Era Antiques here in Concord has told my husband and me of your interest in the porcelain clock that we purchased from him some time ago.'' The woman sounded elderly. She spoke slowly and her hesitant voice was marked with a foreign accent. ''I'd like to ask you a few questions concerning your connection with this clock. If you wouldn't mind, that is.''

Abby's heart was racing with excitement. She was actually speaking with the people who had her clock. She'd hoped so that this would happen, but in her heart she'd really never expected that it would. At the very least it was a minor miracle. ''Of course I wouldn't mind, Mrs. Halpern. I do appreciate your calling, and I'm more than happy to answer any and all questions.'' Abby's animated voice mirrored her enthusiastic delight at receiving this hoped-for call.

''Good—very, very good,'' the older woman said, in her odd guttural voice. ''I understand the clock belonged to your grandmother. Is that correct?''

''Oh yes. It was her most treasured possession. She loved that clock.''

''Can you tell me how she obtained the clock, and possibly when and where she got it?'' Again Abby heard that note of hesitancy in her voice.

''I don't know all the particulars I'm afraid, but I remember Grandmother telling me when I was only twelve or so, that someone gave it to her about the time she finished college. And then she told me that she was going to give it to me when I graduated from college.'' Abby paused and gave a little sigh. ''She died while I was still in high school, but she left me the clock as she had promised.''

''Do you remember how old your grandmother was when she died?''

''I believe she was seventy-two. I know I was sixteen the year she died, and that was eight years ago.''

''This is most interesting to me.'' A different sound had come into Gerda's voice, a note of expectancy, or even wonderment. ''Tell me, dear, what was your grandmother's name?''

''It was Abigail Hampton. And that's my name too. I was named after her, but I've always been called just Abby.''

There was a long moment of silence before Gerda Halpern spoke again. When she did, she sounded somewhat emotional, eager and excited. ''I have only one more question for you Abby,'' she said. ''And I hope it's one you can answer yes to.'' She gave a little, tremulous sigh. ''Was Abigail's maiden name Carlington, and did she come from Savannah, Georgia?''

Dumbfounded, Abby gasped in astonishment. ''Yes—but how in the world did you find that out? I— I mean—is it possible that you knew my grandmother?''

''I met her once,'' Gerda answered, wistfully. ''It was in Vienna—many, many years ago. But that's a long story. One that I think you'll be interested in hearing, and one that I'd like very much to tell you.''

''This is so incredible I hardly know what to say. But of course, I'm terrifically interested in hearing about your meeting my grandmother.''

''It's about much more than our meeting. It's the story about how she came to have the clock. So, my husband Hans and I would like you to come to our home in Concord and let us tell you about it. Will you do that?''

''Oh my, yes. Of course I will. I'll come as soon as you'd like. Tomorrow even, or whenever it's convenient.''

They talked a few more minutes, setting up the day and time for Abby to drive down to Concord. As she hung up the phone, her mind was still reeling from the impact of this unusual conversation with Gerda Halpern. Abby heaved a sigh of relief, however, because the day after tomorrow had been agreed on for her visit. She believed it would have killed her to have had to wait any longer than that.

Abby left the shop and walked half a block to Sally's Kitchen, a small café that served soup and sandwiches. As she ate her lunch, she played back through her mind the conversation she'd just had. There was an aura of mystery about it that piqued her curiosity and certainly intrigued her. This unusual woman, who spoke with a foreign-sounding inflection in her voice, had said some most interesting things. Perhaps the most surprising of which was what she'd said about having met Abby's grandmother in Vienna. Abby shook her head, a perplexed frown narrowing her eyes. When was her grandmother in Vienna? Abby couldn't remember ever having heard her mention anything about Austria, or any place outside of the United States for that matter. Surely if she'd spent any time in a foreign country she would have talked about it. Wouldn't she?

Abby took another bite of her bacon and tomato sandwich, chewing thoughtfully. It was interesting that Gerda Halpern knew that Abigail's name had been Carlington, and that she was born and raised in Savannah, Georgia. That had to mean that she'd met Abigail before she was married to Randall Hampton. But where did the porcelain clock fit into all of this, she wondered. She realized speculating about it was getting her no place. So she put her curiosity on hold and concentrated on finishing her lunch. . . .

That evening she told Rome about the call she'd received and her plans to see the Halpern's. "Why don't you let me drive you down to Concord? I'd really like to," he said.

"Oh, that would be great, but do you really think you can get away from the filming for a whole day?" She looked up at him, a questioning frown narrowing her eyes.

Rome bobbed his head affirmatively. "Sure, no problem. I'll clear it with Jacoby when I get back to the inn tonight. But everything is set for the scenes they're going to wrap up for the rest of this week. They can do without me just fine."

"It's a deal, then." She crossed her arms and relaxed against the cushioned back of the sofa where she and Rome sat together sharing a bowl of buttered popcorn. "You know that fancy car you've been leasing will certainly be more comfortable to travel in than my scruffy old Blazer. Besides, I'll be happy to have some company."

"*Some* company, you say." He eyed her wryly. "That sounds like any old guy would suit you. Maybe I'll see if Drew is free to go with you," Rome said facetiously.

"Don't you dare mention one word of this to Drew," Abby said, raising her voice and glaring at him. "You know very well that it's *your* company that I meant."

"So I just wanted to hear you say it. You can't blame me for that." He leaned over and fed her a fluffy kernel of popcorn, all the time looking at her with a smile as warm as summer in his eyes.

Chapter Fourteen

That time of the year it's especially enjoyable to drive anywhere in the state. For autumn in New Hampshire is always lovely, with the magnificent colors of the turning leaves, blazing bronze, scarlet red, and magenta brown. Other signs of mid to late September are the departure of the swallows, the buckets of blackberries, and often the smell of autumn bonfires.

All but the bonfires were present that morning as Abby and Rome drove leisurely from Lindenwood down to Concord. They had started out early so they could stop at a charming little café in Woodstock for breakfast. Gerda Halpern had asked Abby to come between ten-thirty and eleven, and since they'd located the Halperns' home with no difficulties, they arrived a few minutes before eleven.

Framed by maple trees, the Halperns' white clapboard house was enclosed by an attractive white painted fence. As Abby climbed out of Rome's sports car, a smallish black dog wormed his way through the partially open gate and came to greet them. He was of no known breed, but his rough coat gleamed with good health and he was obviously happy to welcome them. He pranced around Abby, uttering little yelps of pleasure. As she stooped to rub his head, he licked her cheek affectionately.

Rome pushed the gate all the way open, and he and Abby walked up to the front door with the little dog following close at their heels.

The house was a fine example of Colonial Revival style. The impressive front door was painted a dark forest green as were the shutters at each side of the numerous windows. In the center of the door was a shield-shaped brass door knocker that had the name Halpern engraved on it.

''Are you certain you want me to come in with you?'' Rome asked, grabbing her hand as she started reaching for the knocker. ''If you feel it would be easier to talk to these folks alone, I'll wait for you in the car, and I won't mind one bit.''

Abby shook her head. ''No. I need moral support on this. I'm counting on you to help me convince them to let me buy my clock back.''

''Let's have a go at it then,'' he said, immediately lifting the brass knocker and vigorously tapping it three times.

There was only a brief delay before the heavy door swung open, and they were met and cordially welcomed by the Halperns. Hans was a tall man whose military bearing defied his eighty-odd years. However, he did have a heavily lined face and his hair and neatly trimmed beard were the color of sand mixed with snow. Abby judged Gerda to be only slightly younger than her husband. Her face was somewhat wrinkled and its contours blurred by age, but it showed traces of a former beauty, and the azure color of her eyes and the pretty shape of her mouth were pleasing.

The four of them exchanged introductions. Gerda then led them into an attractive living room, charmingly furnished with a mixture of eighteenth- and nineteenth-century antiques, which included an elaborately carved rosewood grand piano, on top of which lay a violin and bow. There was sheet music open on the piano and on the nearby brass music stand, as if in readiness to be played. Abby wondered if it was Gerda or Hans who was the musician in the family, or if perhaps they both were.

Gerda directed Abby to sit with her on the rose-brocade camelback sofa, at the same time indicating that Hans and Rome should take two nearby chairs that formed them into a nice conversational group.

It was only after they were all seated that Abby had a good view of the marble fireplace with its ivory-painted Adam-style mantel. ''Oh, how lovely,'' Abby exclaimed, noticing the exquisite china clock setting in the center of the mantelpiece. It contained a beautiful figure of a girl in a flower-encrusted gown standing at one side of the clock, and nestled at her feet were two baby lambs. ''What a fabulous clock. It reminds me a lot of my grandmother's. The coloring is the same, though hers has the shepherd boy sitting on top, and this one has a girl at the side. Still, with the dog at his feet and the lambs beside her, they are similar. Don't you think so?'' Abby asked, turning a questioning gaze to Gerda.

''Indeed they are. More than just similar. That's what I brought you here to show you,'' she said, an enigmatic smile in her eyes. ''You see, Abby, the two clocks were specially designed and created together— as a unique pair.''

Abby was more than a little puzzled. ''Do you mean that this clock of yours and the one my grandmother had were some sort of commissioned art pieces?''

''I mean exactly that,'' Gerda answered.

''Ah,'' Hans interjected, clearing his throat. ''And you've never seen anyone as excited as my wife was the afternoon she and I walked into the Golden Era shop and saw the clock that had been given to your relative. Gerda hadn't seen Fritz's clock in over fifty years. She just stood there staring at it and crying. Poor Mott Collins didn't know what to make of it. Told me later that he'd had customers give delighted sighs, whistle, even shout with joy over an antique find, but he'd never had someone cry her heart out like Gerda did.''

''Well, I had every right to be emotional. Seeing that clock again brought back a flood of memories,'' Gerda admonished her husband with a show of feminine indignation. So you be quiet now, Hans, because Abby needs to know the whole story of the clocks, starting at the very beginning.'' Gerda turned to Abby and smiled. ''I know you and Mr. Douglas must be very curious about all of this.''

Abby nodded. ''Yes we are. And I'm confused too.'' She pressed her hand to her lips, wagging her head in bewilderment. ''All these years I believed the shepherd clock was my grandmother's. Now your husband called it Fritz's clock. Who—who is Fritz?''

''Fritz was my brother—my twin brother,'' Gerda answered.

''And the clocks were made for the two of you. Of course, that explains why one of the clocks has a shepherd and the other a shepherdess,'' Abby reflected, speaking softly and more to herself than to anyone else. She had her head lowered, so now she raised it, looking into Gerda's face. ''Were you born in Austria, you and your twin?''

''Oh yes, in Vienna,'' Gerda exclaimed proudly. ''The Zoeller family all lived in Vienna for three generations.''

''Karl Zoeller was a well-known textile manufacturer,'' Hans said, adding his bit to his wife's family background.

''Abby's not interested in Papa's business, Hans,'' Gerda chided him. ''She wants to hear about the clocks.'' She paused just long enough to draw a breath. ''Papa intended for them to be made in time to commemorate our first birthdays, but he discovered that artists, makers of fine china, and skilled watch technicians all create slowly. Fritz and I got our clocks when we were three. Even at that young age we both sensed that they were unique gifts. Ones we would both cherish all of our lives.'' There was a note of nostalgia in her quiet voice, and for an instant a wistfulness stole into her expression. ''Now you know how the two clocks came to be, and you know who Fritz was. But I expect there's another part of this story that you're more interested in hearing; I'm guessing that you're curious to learn how Fritz and Abigail met. I'm sure too, that you'd like to know why he wished to give his treasured clock to her.''

''You bet I'm curious about that. To tell you the truth, you gave me the surprise of my life when you said you'd met my grandmother in Vienna. That is so strange. I still can't believe that as much as my grandmother loved that clock, and as many times as she talked to me about it, she never mentioned the person who gave it to her. And I certainly never heard anything about her having been in Europe.''

''Well, she was only there for such a brief time,'' Gerda said, sighing sadly. ''Perhaps what happened to her there became a bittersweet memory too precious to share.''

''I suppose so,'' Abby agreed thoughtfully. ''I simply never thought of her as a young, romantic girl before. Apparently, that's exactly what she was when you met her. Tell me when that was, won't you? And how she came to be in Vienna?''

''It was 1937, a highly critical time for much of Europe. Of course we didn't know it, but in less than a year German troops would march in and occupy Austria.'' An abject look of sadness passed over her features. She sighed, clasped her heavily veined hands together, and continued. ''It was June as I recall, and it seems Abigail had just graduated from one of your women's colleges. She and several other graduates, under the supervision of their art instructor from the college, were on a tour of museums and art galleries in Paris, Florence, Amsterdam, and Vienna. I believe those were the different cities.''

Abby's face lighted up with interest. ''That would have been why she came, of course. I should have guessed it was something like that. It's always been a popular thing for college graduates to take a tour of Europe following college and before they go out and get a job. It's the in thing to do, if your parents can afford it, that is,'' she added, laughing. ''Also, Grandmother was into art and art history. She even took painting lessons when she was young, and then again after she was married. She was pretty good too,'' Abby said, turning her head quickly to look at Rome. ''You know that painting of a road lined with big oak trees draped with Spanish moss that hangs in the small back parlor at Hampton House?'' she asked him. She

paused, peering at him, waiting to see a flicker of rec-
ognition in his expression.

"It hangs over the fireplace, doesn't it?"

"Yes, that's it. Abigail painted it."

"Well, it's good. Those moss-covered trees add a
touch of the old South to that early New England
home of yours that's charming. As a matter of fact,
there's a scene in our movie that's played in front of
that fireplace, so you'll see some good shots of that
painting."

"Gee, I'm glad to hear that." She flashed Rome a
pleased smile. "I should explain to Hans and you,
Gerda, that Rome is with Allied movie studios. Right
now they're making a picture in Lindenwood, and
some of it has been filmed inside my house."

"I'd like very much to hear about this movie you're
making," Hans said, a look of eager interest lighting
his pale eyes. "Why don't we take leave of the ladies
and go to the library where we can talk about your
work and Gerda and Abby can go on with their rem-
iniscing. You won't mind if we do that, will you,
dear?" He addressed these last words to his wife as
he rose from his chair.

Gerda's eyes crinkled in an understanding smile.
"Not at all. Go along you two. We'll join you in just
a little while." She waved the two of them off blithely.
She waited until they were out of the room before
adding. "I'm surprised they hung around as long as
they did. Certainly Hans jumped at the chance for

some man talk." She chuckled good-naturedly. "Bless his heart. I know he's weary of hearing these stories out of the past."

"But they are new to me, and I'm fascinated to discover these things about my grandmother that I've never known before. So please, go on. Tell me about your brother and my grandmother."

"Fritz always said that it was preordained that they would meet and fall in love, that they were two people meant for each other."

"That's a lovely thought, and wonderfully romantic, certainly."

Gerda smiled. "Yes, but if you'd seen them together, as I did, you would believe it was true."

Made for each other—wasn't that just in fairy tales? A slight smile traced Abby's lips. "But their first meeting. How did it happen?" she asked, wanting to fit all the pieces together.

"The way Fritz explains it, that was when destiny stepped into both of their lives. It just happened that the leader of Abigail's tour group became ill the first night she and the girls arrived in Vienna. The following morning, therefore, the hotel arranged for the girls to take a tour of Vienna on one of the regular sightseeing buses. As luck would have it, however, Abigail was several minutes late coming down to the lobby where the group was to meet, so the bus left without her."

"I can believe Grandmother arrived too late," Abby

said in an amused voice. "Southern girls are renowned for their slow, drawling way of speaking and for their tardiness. And I have to tell you that all the years she lived and raised a family up here among brisk-talking, fast-paced New Englanders didn't change her very much." Abby gave a verbal shrug. "I didn't mean to interrupt. Please go on," she said. And to show that she was going to be quiet and listen, Abby crossed her arms, settled back in a comfortable position and focused her full attention on this kindly Austrian woman, whose brother had once known and loved her grandmother.

"Fritz just happened to be at the hotel that morning for a business meeting. As he was leaving, he overheard Abigail attempting to see if the desk clerk could tell her where she could go to catch up with the tour bus. Of course, Abigail couldn't speak German, and the clerk, though he spoke some English, couldn't understand her excited outpouring of words. Fritz stepped in to offer assistance, saying he'd be happy to drive her around to the places of interest in the city and possibly they would meet up with her group. They didn't locate her friends, however. This fact didn't surprise me," Gerda said, a twinkle in her eyes. "I think that was a deliberate act on Fritz's part, because he wished to keep Abigail to himself. Naturally he never admitted that to me." She gave a knowing chuckle. "And after that first day, Fritz spent every waking moment while Abigail was in Vienna with her."

Gerda smiled and shrugged. "Like you Americans always say—the rest is history."

Abby was totally intrigued by this love story about her grandmother. It sounded like a lovely romance, the kind that they used to make into a touching movie. "You haven't told me yet about the clock. I'm dying to know when Fritz gave it to her. Do tell me everything you remember about that."

"Oh, I remember that night very well indeed. It was the evening before Abigail was to leave Vienna. Fritz brought her to our home to meet the family. It was truly a memorable occasion. Mother saw to it that everything would be perfect, because we all knew by then that Fritz was deeply in love with this pretty, poised, and utterly charming American girl. My parents were concerned because Fritz and Abigail had known each other for such a short time. But all doubts vanished when they met her. For all of us could see that her love for him was as great as his for her. So you see, Fritz giving Abigail his clock was not only a symbol of his total commitment to her, but in a special way it conveyed the blessing of his family." She paused, rubbing her hand slowly back and forth across her wrinkled forehead. There was a faraway look in her eyes as if she were gazing back at that long-ago scene. She remained quiet for a long moment. "We were all so very happy that night," she murmured finally. "The future seemed bright with promise. None of us realized then how drastically the war would alter all of our lives.''

Hearing the pathos in Gerda's voice, Abby reached out her hand to her in a gesture of sympathy. ''My grandmother never saw Fritz again, did she.'' It was more a statement than a question. ''How sad for both of them.''

''Many things changed in Vienna after that summer. And I'll tell you quickly and end my story,'' Gerda said, giving Abby's hand an affectionate squeeze. ''A few weeks before the German occupation of Austria took place, Papa sent Mother and me to Switzerland, to Mother's relatives. We tried to take as many of our treasured things with us as we could. That's why I still have my own clock, and I'm certain that if Abigail hadn't taken Fritz's clock back to the States with her, his clock would have been destroyed, or at least lost to us forever.''

''What about your father and Fritz?''

''They stayed in Vienna because our home, Papa's business, everything he'd worked so hard for was in Austria, and all of his employees counted on him to keep the factories running. I think they believed he could somehow protect them and their jobs from the Germans—and he did for about a year.''

''What happened then?''

Gerda clasped her frail hands together and stared at them as she answered. ''We were never told exactly what took place—only that Papa and Fritz were killed. Shot down outside one of the Zoeller textile mills by three uniformed men. Just two of the countless victims of the brutal war.'' She sighed heavily, her voice filled with anguish.

Before Abby could utter a sympathetic comment, Gerda got up from the sofa. ''I've talked enough about the past, and now I want you to come with me and see your shepherd clock again,'' she said, gesturing for Abby to follow her.

Abby jumped up and together they walked across the hall into a formal dining room beautifully furnished with a Queen Anne pedestal table, Chippendale-style chairs, and a two-tiered brass chandelier. An imposing mahogany buffet spanned a side wall, in the center of which was the antique clock that Fritz had given to her grandmother, flanked by a pair of exquisite floral-pattern porcelain urns.

''What a beautiful dining room,'' Abby exclaimed, fingering the smooth mellow wood surface of the buffet. ''And certainly a perfect setting to display your treasured things.''

''They're not all mine, you know,'' the older woman said, in her soft, hesitant voice. ''Hans and I understand from Mr. Collins that you never intended for the clock to be sold. He explained the unfortunate circumstances that caused you to lose it, and of course, that's why we felt we should see you and talk to you about it.''

"Oh, and you can't know how much I appreciate that. All the things that you've told me today—it means so—so much—"

"Shhh, don't talk." Gerda held her hand palm out toward Abby. "Let me finish what I want to say. You see, now that we have met you, I can see that the clock means a lot to you, and also I realize Abigail wanted you to have it." She paused, moving her shoulders in a gesture of resignation. "What I'm trying to say is that Hans and I certainly intend to let you take the clock back."

Gerda's words touched Abby. How generous this dear woman was and how sensitive to others' feelings. Abby thought of the sacrifice Gerda was willing to make. After all, it was her brother's clock they were talking about. And Fritz was even closer to Gerda than a brother, for he was her twin—her counterpart. Unexpectedly, Abby's throat tightened and she felt tears gathering behind her eyes. She thought of what Hans had said earlier about his wife's reaction at finding her brother's clock in the antique store. How she stood there, staring at it and crying her heart out. . . .

These thoughts and the tragic story that Gerda had revealed to her today seemed to spin around and around in her head, telling her there was one answer, one thing only that was right for her to do. So she smiled softly at Gerda and stepped forward, closing the space between them. She laid her hand gently on Gerda's arm. "I know that my grandmother would feel, as I do, that the place where Fritz's clock belongs is right here in this beautiful room. And so it is here that it shall remain with you.'' Abby spoke firmly, with the sense of conviction that was part of her character.

A luminous smile warmed the older woman's parchmentlike face. ''Thank you, Abigail,'' she said softly, as two silent tears spilled out of her eyes and ran down her cheeks.

Chapter Fifteen

As they started the drive back to Lindenwood, Abby related the touching story about her grandmother and Fritz Zoeller. Then she explained to Rome why she'd made the decision she had concerning the antique clock.

"Are you sure you're okay with this?" he asked, not masking his concern for her feelings.

"I'm sure," she responded.

"Good," he said.

Abby was grateful that Rome did not pursue the subject, but lapsed into silence. He seemed to be sensitive to her emotional state. This to her was a blessing, for at the moment she desired nothing more than to just ride along quietly, gazing out the window and not having to think or talk about anything. It was a beautiful afternoon. Abby was aware of the golden autumn shimmer. She could understand why poets talked about days that were made of mellow wine, when the air seemed to tingle with life, the skies were a deeper blue, and the grass had caught all colors of leaves. The turn to autumn is an event of nature, but it's also a passage whose beginning can be detected by the listening heart.

For the next ten or fifteen miles they drove in companionable silence. Finally, when Rome broke into Abby's reverie, oddly enough his words echoed her thoughts about the season.

"It's great to be out on the road this time of year," he said. "The leaves are spectacular. Are they always like this?"

"The last week of September and the first week of October they are. The natives hereabouts swear that the fall season in New England is second to none. It doesn't get better than this."

Rome laughed. "I'll buy that."

"You don't have to, it's free," she countered glibly. "So make the most of it."

"I intend to. But you've got to do it with me. Will you?" He took his eyes off the road long enough to look at her for some sign of agreement.

"I might. Depends on what you have in mind."

"Well, you know, of course, that the Highland Games are taking place at the end of next week. I want to take you to see every event. We won't miss a single thing." His voice crescendoed with enthusiasm. "It'll be a great weekend."

"But didn't you tell me that Jacoby expected to finish up *A Different Drummer* by next Monday or Tuesday?" she asked, staring at Rome's profile, a confused frown on her face.

"Yeah, that's right."

"But if they've finished filming, won't you be on your way back to Hollywood with the others?"

"No way! What kind of Scotsman would miss such an event as the Gathering of the Scottish Clans?" he asked with fierce ardor.

"Not your kind, obviously," Abby said, an amused smile crinkling the corners of her eyes. "And believe me, I'm going to love tagging right along with you."

Rome warned Abby that the final days of a location shoot would move at a hectic pace. Certainly this proved true for him. In the days that followed, Rome seemed to have to be in two different places at the same time. The result was that Abby scarcely saw him.

Jacoby had called it right on the nose, for they wrapped up their filming in Hampton House on Monday. The following day they moved out all their equipment. Then Allied sent in a cleaning crew to get Abby's house in pristine shape, and everything arranged back exactly the way she wanted it. While Abby was at her house supervising this, Rome was with Jacoby, Brent, and the stars of *A Different Drummer*, filming the few remaining outdoor scenes that Jacoby wanted shot against a background of brilliant fall foliage.

All of this was accomplished by late Wednesday, and by early afternoon on Thursday, the director, actors, camera crews, and production staff, with the exception of Rome, had all left Lindenwood.

Of course, Abby was glad that Rome was staying in Lindenwood through the weekend for the Highland Games. It gave her two extra days to spend with him. Time she would cherish and remember always. Also, it meant that at least her June through September romance with the Scotsman was going to come to an end on a gala occasion. Who knows? Maybe amidst the traditional Scottish songs, lively dancing, the skirl of the bagpipes, and the sound of the drums and bands, she wouldn't realize her heart was breaking.

Friday morning, Abby searched through her closet for something appropriate to wear to the opening ceremonies. Though she certainly didn't expect Rome to show up wearing a kilt, still, in his enthusiasm for this event she had no doubts but that he'd let it be known in some way that he wasn't called the Scotsman without good cause. She scooted hangers along the clothes rod until she came to a red and green plaid jumper. She paired it with a white turtleneck and decided it wasn't a bad outfit at all.

When Rome came to pick her up, he was wearing navy blue slacks, a white shirt, and an argyle jacket bearing a Scottish crest which undoubtedly was that of the Douglas clan. Now Abby knew what it was he'd ordered from the Scottish import shop.

"You make a right bonny lassie, Abby girl," he

said, admiring her from head to toe with obvious approval.

"And you're a bold, handsome laddie," she countered, looping her arm through his as they walked out to his car.

A large crowd was rapidly gathering at the parade grounds by the time Rome and Abby arrived at Loon Mountain. Rome grabbed a firm hold of her hand as they joined the throng of people filling up the bleachers.

Once they got seated fairly near the center, they waited only about ten minutes before the massed pipes and drums led by three guest bands began marching in. In their regimental regalia, they made a splendid sight and a stirring sound.

"They're awesome!" Abby exclaimed, her voice rising.

"You can say that again," Rome agreed, sounding as excited as she did.

They marched on and took position on the parade ground. Then the governor of New Hampshire, the chieftain of the games, and the other honored guests took their places on the reviewing stand. In this impressive formation, the national anthems of the participating countries were presented: "God Save the Queen," "O Canada," "The Star-Spangled Banner," and "The Flower of Scotland." Abby wasn't the only one whose emotions were affected by these stirring salutes to England, Canada, the United States, and

Scotland. Rome stood close at her side, an enrapt expression on his strong-boned face.

Following the anthems, the massed bands played a salute to this year's Chieftain of the Highland Games, after which the VIP introductions were made, and the bands marched in their honor. At this point, the chieftain declared the Highland Games open, and the bands performed a final march and countermarch for the chieftain, and then the proceedings were closed.

"I can't understand, when you live so close to Loon Mountain, why you've never been to the Highland Games before," Rome said, as they moved slowly along with the crowd as they were leaving the parade area.

"I don't know either," Abby answered, shrugging one shoulder. "I guess because no one offered to take me till now." She angled her head up at him and smiled. "But you're called the Scotsman, and you've never seen any Scottish games before either. I guess we're both finding out what we've been missing."

"Right—and I like the idea that we're seeing it for the first time together." He put his arm around her shoulders and led her off to one side. "Now let's stop for a minute and choose which event we want to pick out to see this morning."

"You said we were going to see them all."

"Well, I discovered we can't do that."

"Why not?" she challenged him, jutting her chin out at a stubborn angle.

"Because three or four things go on at the same time. So let's take a look at the schedule and see what's up for this hour and select the one we want to see most." He pulled a folded sheet of paper out of his inside coat pocket, opened it, and studied it for a second. "Okay, Abby," he said, scratching his head thoughtfully. "It looks like we have four things to choose from: a tartan seminar, a genealogical lecture, a Gaelic music workshop, or the sheepdog trials."

Abby smiled inwardly at Rome's recital of events. For though he made a noble effort to show he had an open mind about it, he did grimace slightly over some of the possible choices. So she couldn't resist a temptation to have some fun with it. "Well now," she said, feigning total seriousness, "since I'm not Scottish, I'll pass on the tartan bit. Unless, of course, it's really important to you."

"No, it's not," he assured her, shaking his head. "I'll go along with whatever you pick. That'll suit me fine."

Abby continued to frown thoughtfully. "Genealogy is out for me too. It would be interesting, I guess, but I'm not really into it." She thought Rome didn't look at all disappointed to hear this. "So, that leaves Gaelic music or the sheepdogs." Once more she pretended to ponder the options carefully before announcing her decision. "You know," she said finally, "I know the Gaelic music would be very entertaining—but what I'd really like to do is watch the dog trials."

"I'd go for that too." Rome flashed a gleeful smile, and though he'd probably deny it, Abby knew he was relieved.

She pressed her lips together to hide a mischievous smile as they walked away from the parade grounds and headed for the Loon Mountain Athletic Field, where the heavy athletic events and the sheepdog trials were being held.

The large, partially fenced-off area where a large number of dogs with their owners were assembling, was a field adjoining some hilly terrain. A herd of sheep were huddled at one side, and on the other several large tents had been set up. Abby and Rome approached what appeared to be the main tent involved in this particular event. A robust young man in Highland dress, an official badge pinned to his jacket, was gathering up the spectators and a group of what Abby judged to be a class of seventh- or eighth-grade students, probably from one of the middle schools in Lincoln or North Woodstock.

"If all of you will move in close enough to hear me, I'll tell you about the dogs, and explain the format of the competition," he said, speaking in a voice that marked him as a Brit, and probably one from Yorkshire in northern England.

"Come on, Rome. I want to hear this," Abby said, edging closer.

"I should tell you first that while this competition is open to all types of sheepdogs, most of the dogs you'll be seeing today are Border collies. And I'm proud to say that the Border collie breed was developed quite some years ago by shepherds in Britain who were attempting to find the perfect sheepdog.'' A smile split his rugged face as he said this. ''And they certainly did,'' he added. ''These dogs are intelligent, obedient, eager to please, easily trained, and have a strong natural instinct to herd. However, they have no standard of appearance for the breed. Border collies vary in color, length of coat, and size. Their weight can run from thirty to over sixty pounds.''

The young man stopped talking for a few minutes to allow some latecomers to join their group. ''Now the competition will begin in just a few minutes,'' he continued, once the new people were close enough to hear him. ''Each dog will attempt to run four sheep through five obstacles on the course. Each sheep is worth five points, and a perfect run earns one hundred points. The format will be that all the dogs will run once, and then the top ten qualifiers will rerun to establish the top ten places.''

''This is going to be exciting to watch,'' Abby said, as she and Rome located a good viewing spot behind the fence.

''Hey, look over there.'' Rome pointed to where the owners were assembled with their dogs. ''Several of those guys must be entering more than one dog. They've got a leash in each hand.''

Abby looked in the direction he'd indicated. ''And

some of those guys happen to be gals,'' she told him, squinting her eyes to see their faces better. ''That redhead in the green bomber jacket is definitely female, and she's got two dogs, a black and white and one that looks kind of reddish. This is definitely not an all-male contest.''

''I didn't say it was,'' Rome defended himself, shaking his head at her. ''I'll even concede that the dogs aren't all of the male gender either.'' He gave a broad wink. ''Although, if I were a shepherd I'd bet I'd find a male dog easier to handle. What do you think?''

''I think I'd like to change the subject.''

''Coward,'' Rome taunted her, his mouth quirking with humor.

''Chauvinist,'' she countered, barely able to keep the laughter out of her voice.

The sheep and the dogs were fascinating to watch. By the time the top ten were starting the second run, Abby had singled out her two favorites. One was a medium-sized black and white Border collie named Piper, owned by a man with the good Scottish name of MacDuff. The other was a a bit smaller, with a rusty brown and white coat and the name Rosie. Her owner was the attractive redhead in the green jacket who Abby had noticed earlier. Rome had singled out as his favorite a white, shaggy-coated dog with black ears and black around his eyes. It wasn't too surprising that his name was Clown. He turned out to be quite a fa-

vorite of the spectators, too. Though he didn't place
first and get the top money prize of $300, as well as
the perpetual trophy, the coveted silver Campbell Cup,
still Clown did place third and got $200 in prize
money. The dogs Abby favored did not fair quite so
well. Piper placed fifth for $100, and the endearing
little Rosie was ninth and got $50.

It was now mid afternoon, and although the soft
autumn sun dappled the paths that led to the various
food stands and the vendors' area, a light breeze had
come up, putting a chill in the air. So when Rome
suggested that they find one of the places where they
serve fresh-made Scottish scones with piping hot tea,
Abby was highly in favor of it.

Musical entertainment was provided all through the
day in the vendors' area. So while Rome and Abby
were enjoying their tea, they were entertained by a
musician born and raised in Greenock, Scotland. He
strummed his guitar and sang traditional songs of his
homeland, mixing in a few familiar Irish, English, and
American tunes. After twenty minutes or so, he wandered off to another area. Rome looked at his watch
as the singer left, then pulled the events schedule from
his pocket once again.

''You know, Abby, it looks like we have time to
take in a Highland dance exhibition. It's the last thing
on the schedule for this afternoon. You want to try
it?''

''I'm game for anything as long as I can watch it

sitting down. After standing up so long watching those great dogs, I'm ready to sit a while,'' she said, making a grimace.

''I imagine there'll be spectator seats available for this. If there aren't, I promise you we'll leave.''

''No, we won't,'' she said, then paused long enough to drain the last drop of tea from her cup. ''I will not let it be said that I kept a member of the clan of Douglas from seeing the Highland Fling,'' she added, shoving her chair back and getting to her feet.

Rome stood up too. ''Not to mention the legendary Scottish Sword Dance,'' he said, his eyes meeting hers as they exchanged a subtle look of amusement. . . .

Chapter Sixteen

Abby awakened Saturday morning with her thoughts and emotions jumbled in a crazy quilt of disorder. This was to be the last day she would spend with Rome. She wondered how in the world she would be able to carry it off.

On the one hand, she wanted to leap out of bed, get dressed, and set a whirlwind pace for a final day packed with so much fun and excitement that she wouldn't have time to think about tomorrow, when Rome would be gone.

On the other hand, she wanted to delay the dawn, have the hours crawl by slowly, and make this precious time with him last as long as possible.

But then again, what she really needed to do was to pray for this day to pass. Have it over and done with before her resolve crumbled and she broke down and let Rome find out that what was meant to be only a light, carefree, summer romance between them had become much more than that for her.

As she threw back the covers and got out of bed, she wondered if she could hide the depth of her feelings for Rome through this one final day. She tossed her head, lifting her chin at a stubborn angle. She could—and she must.

The heavy athletic competitions are highly popular events at the Highland Games. Abby hadn't been too sure that they would appeal tremendously to her, but Rome's obvious enthusiasm was starting to rub off on her as they arrived at an athletic field swarming with spectators. It was soon apparent that many of the athletes had their own group of fans, for as the competitor's name and the country he came from was announced, there was much cheering and applause.

"I think there were two from Nova Scotia and at least three from Ontario," Abby commented. "Now I know why they sang 'O Canada' at the opening ceremony yesterday."

"Sounded like our Eastern states are well represented too. I heard them call out Maine, New York, and New Hampshire a number of times."

"That's good. We've got to show that we grow our men just as big and strong as they do in the provinces."

Rome eyed her wryly. "Well, wherever these good Scottish clansmen hail from, if they're taking part in today's events, they'll all be long on brawn and stout of heart."

"You're right, of course," Abby said with a demure smile. "So lead the way, and let's go where all the action is."

She took the hand Rome offered, and the two of them proceeded to an area where two high poles with a bar stretched between them stood. To Abby they looked like goalposts on a football field. A swarthy man was standing facing the crowd, with his back to the goalposts. He held a pitchfork in his hands while two other men were placing some gunnysack-covered material on the ground near him.

''What's this all about?'' Abby asked.

''It's called the sheaf toss,'' Rome told her.

''Are those things the sheafs?'' Abby asked, pointing to the gunnysacks.

Rome nodded. ''Those are sixteen pounds of hay wrapped in burlap. That fellow standing there is going to pick one up on his pitchfork, and toss it over his shoulder and over the bar. Each contestant gets three tosses at each height. The bar is raised six inches at a time until all but one man is eliminated.''

This didn't sound all that intriguing to Abby, but once it got underway, she was surprised at how fascinating it proved to be. Loud cheers went up from the audience when the toss was successful, sighs and groans when a toss failed. As the bar was raised and competitors were eliminated, the excitement elevated to a fever pitch. The ultimate winner was surrounded by a storm of applause.

The weight toss that followed was a somewhat similar event which also used the tall poles and the bar.

Again the contestant stands with his back to the poles. He then picks up a fifty-six-pound weight, swings it between his knees, then, using only one hand, tosses it over the bar. Three misses or touches at the same height means elimination, and the highest toss wins.

Then they announced that there would be a weight Throw, a tug-of-war event, and something called the stone carry. These popular games lead up to the final and most popular event of the Highland Games, the spectacular caber toss.

Now each of these various acivites takes considerable time, and as Rome obviously was not inclined to miss a minute of it, Abby willingly offered to go seek out one of the food vendors and get them some lunch. She really didn't mind forgoing watching herculean men handles stone boulders. Such feats of great physical strength didn't hold the same appeal for women as they did for men. So Abby took her time wandering through the food tents until she found a jolly vendor in a butcher's apron serving spicy-smelling barbecued beef sandwiches on large, round, sesame-seed buns. She asked him to wrap two to go, bought two iced colas, and headed back to the athletic field.

It was the end of the afternoon when the time came for the traditional caber toss. *Caber* is the Gaelic word for rafter or pole. The caber toss involves grabbing hold from a crouched position of the caber, standing upright while still holding the pole, moving forward, and then attempting to toss it end over end.

"That looks like a telephone pole," Abby said when she saw the caber. "How long is it, anyway?"

"I understand it's approximately eighteen feet long and weighs somewhere between one hundred twenty and one hundred eighty pounds."

"And you mean to tell me a man can pick it up from its base, and not only move forward with it but then flip it end over end?" She shook her head. "That's hard to believe."

"Well, you're going to see the first fellow try right now." Rome pointed to a redheaded and bearded fellow walking forward when they called out the familiar Scottish name of MacDonald. He was well known to the crowd of spectators, for cheers went up and cries of "Show 'em how it's done, Red!"

The caber toss was an incredible feat to view. As one man followed another, each one displayed tremendous strength, stamina, and agility. Abby's cheers were as loud and enthusiastic as anyone's, and her clapping vigorous. The result was that by the end of the day, the palms of her hands were rosy red and her voice sounded like a rusty foghorn.

They left the field then and headed toward the parking area, where Rome had left his car. "I found out that there's something special going on around here tonight called 'The Flavor of Scotland.' Have you heard about it?'' Rome asked, as he guided her through the rows of cars.

Abby shrugged. ''I don't think so. What is it?''

''Well, it seems that a number of the local restaurants in nearby Lincoln and North Woodstock are featuring special Scottish menus in honor of the Highland Games. I heard they're having haggis, venison, game birds, maybe even rabbit. Want to try some true Scottish fare?''

''Sure do.'' Abby's answer was quick and uttered with much enthusiasm.

''Good. You're my kind of girl, Abby.'' He chuckled and gave her a sly wink. ''That's why I made us reservations for six-thirty in North Woodstock.''

Knowing from experience that Rome never failed to gauge his time precisely, she was not surprised when they arrived at the inn at six-twenty-five and were seated at their table in an attractive windowed area of the dining room at exactly six-thirty. Aware that one of the best known Scottish dishes was haggis, she was certain that Rome would choose it. But being less adventuresome than he, Abby decided on the roast grouse, which was garnished with watercress and served with port wine gravy and red currant jelly.

''This tastes elegant,'' Abby said, enjoying her savory food.

''The haggis is excellent too. I want you to try it.'' He pushed his plate over so she could take some.

She waved it away, wrinkling her nose in distaste. "I don't think so, Rome. I've read a recipe for haggis, and I know it's made of the liver, heart, and other parts of a sheep. I'll just pass on that."

He frowned at her. "Abby you have to try at least one bite. I'm going to have to insist on that." His tone was stern, and he was eyeing her intently. "How can I take you to Scotland with me if you won't even try to eat the Scots' most famous dish?"

Abby stared at him, bemused. Why would Rome be saying this to her? "I—I thought you were taking a California gal with you when you went to Scotland. In fact, I remember you saying that."

"Oh no, Abby. You were the one that mentioned California. I didn't." His eyes never wavered from hers as he said this. "I said that I wanted to find a pretty lassie to take with me to Scotland. I didn't mention where I hoped I might find her."

Was Rome deliberately teasing her, she wondered. Surely he was putting her on with all this talk about taking her with him to Scotland. But if it was all a joke, he was making it pretty convincing. Trying to make light of it, Abby took her fork, reached over, and took a small amount of the haggis from his plate and popped it in her mouth like an obedient child. She ate it rather slowly, noting that it had an unusual flavor and a texture something like a pudding made of finely ground meat. The most prominent taste was that of liver.

"How do you like it?" Rome inquired, studying her face closely to see her reaction.

"It's not bad. Kind of unusual, though."

"Yeah, you have to acquire a taste for haggis. Try another bite."

"No, that's enough for right now." She put him off with a gentle smile and immediately resumed eating her own dinner, being careful to keep her eyes lowered to escape Rome's further scrutiny.

They both ate for a time in silence, and when they did resume their conversation, the subject was neither food nor Scotland.

By the time Abby and Rome finished dinner and were leaving the inn, the night air had become so chilled that it made Abby shiver. Rome immediately put his coat around her, and then hugged her shoulders as they walked to his car. Though it was cold, it was still a beautiful night. A big, round harvest moon hung in the sky above their heads right over the bright evening star which swung below it like a locket on a chain.

The drive back to Lindenwood didn't take long at all. In fact, it seemed much too short a time to Abby, for she relished the feeling of sitting at Rome's side as they drove through this September night, this last night they might ever be together.

When they arrived back at Hampton House, Rome took Abby's keys and unlocked the front door. "Abby,

I've got something I need to talk to you about,'' he said, as they went inside. ''You know, for the past two days the only thing we've talked about has been the Highland Games.''

''Well after all, Rome, you'd hardly take me to something as important as the Gathering of the Scottish Clans and expect to talk about the weather, now would you?'' she wisecracked with an impish grin.

''Okay you funny girl. Get serious, because right now I simply want to sit down on one of those stiff-backed, horsehair things you call a Victorian sofa with you beside me, gaze into your eyes, hold your hand, and say what I want to say. Can we just do that, please?''

''All right, but first, it's more of a love seat than a sofa, and it's not horsehair. Besides, if you sit up properly, you'll find it's only mildly uncomfortable,'' Abby said, starting to walk into the living room.

''You will concede that it takes some getting used to, though,'' Rome commented, following after her.

''Then take one of the wing chairs next to the fireplace, they're very comfortable. I'll sit across from you in the other one.''

''But then I can't hold your hand,'' he muttered woefully.

''Well, Rome, you can't have your creature comforts and hold my hand too,'' she said in an amused tone.

At this, Rome grabbed her hand, led her to the sofa,

and gently pushed her to sit down. "You're not helping me out with all this teasing, Abby. I really have something important I want to say."

Heaven knows she was doing everything she could think of to keep things casual and light between them. Make their parting easier for him as well as for her. Why couldn't he see that, she thought as she struggled to think of what she might possibly say to get this all over with. "Okay, I think I can help, Rome. You see, I already know what it is you want to say."

He looked at her in total amazement. "You do!"

"Yes, you want to say good-bye," she said softly, fighting to keep her voice from revealing her emotions.

Rome stared at her, and his eyes seemed to probe to her very soul. "What makes you think I want to say that?" he asked, his expression grave.

"Because you're leaving Lindenwood tomorrow, returning to California, and that means it's time for us to say good-bye." Abby had been preparing herself for this moment, and now that it was here, she managed to speak evenly and sound almost matter-of-fact about it.

"Well now, you're right about my leaving tomorrow, but you're completely wrong about the rest." His voice was calm, and his steady gaze never wavered from her face. "Let me make one thing abundantly clear to you, Abby. I don't want to say good-bye to you—not now, not ever."

Now it was Abby's turn to register surprise. "But Allied's filming is finished here, and you're going back to Hollywood tomorrow—"

"No, I'm not." Rome interrupted her. "I'm going to New York tomorrow. I have an appointment Monday morning with Prentice Lysander, a Broadway producer who wants me to design the sets for his next show." There was excitement in his voice and an expression of satisfaction showed in his eyes.

"Oh Rome, that's wonderful! It's what you've hoped for, and I'm thrilled for you."

"It's a terrific opportunity all right, and I'm happy about it for more reasons than one." He took hold of her hands as he said this, and held them secured in his warm grasp. "You know this means that I'll be staying here on the East Coast where you are Abby, and where I want to be."

Abby's lips were curved in a hesitant smile as though joy had taken her by surprise. "Then this is what you wanted to tell me," she said, a tremor of happiness rippling through her. "And believe me, Rome, you couldn't have told me anything I'd have rather heard."

His earnest eyes sought hers. "You remember that day on the covered bridge when we both made our wishes? Your wish was for me to get the chance to design sets for a Broadway show."

"And happily that wish came true, Rome," she said softly, a tender smile moving across her lips. "I knew it would, you know, because I held my breath the whole way across that long bridge.''

''I held mine all the time until we came out the other side too, Abby. And I want my wish to come true more than I've ever wanted anything in my life. I'll need your help for it to happen, though. Will you make my wish come true?''

Abby's heart was beating with a slow, heavy excitement as she listened to Rome's every word with a growing sense of enchantment. ''I—I'll try. But I don't even know what you wished for. You never told me.''

''I couldn't tell you then, and fortunately you didn't ask.''

''I'm asking now.''

He gave her hands a loving squeeze, then released them. ''And I want very much to tell you now,'' Rome said, leaning toward her, taking her face in his hands, and gently caressing it. ''I wished that the filming of *A Different Drummer* would take as many weeks as possible in order for me to have time to make you fall in love with me. You see I was already head over heels in love with you. I started falling in love with you that very first night when we went to the Foxglove for dinner. You'd found out from Brent that I was called 'the Scotsman,' and right away you began teasing me about my Scottish ways. Then you went home that night and read up on Scottish history and the legendary men of the Douglas clan. You intrigued me, enchanted me, and I adored everything about you. I still do, Abby, and I always will. I love you with all my heart, and more than anything in this world I want to marry you and spend the rest of my life by your side.''

As he said all of this, Rome was looking at her so profoundly, and with such love, that Abby felt wild happiness surging through her. She was filled with triumphant emotion, knowing Rome loved her as she loved him. Her response was swift and joyous. She threw her arms around his neck and kissed him.

When her soft lips touched his, Rome sighed longingly, his arms crushed her against him and his warm mouth moved over hers, ardent with passion, igniting a glorious response inside her.

She moaned against the touch of his mouth exploring the softness of her lips. Then their lips spoke against each other, murmuring, laughing, making small, wordless sounds. When Rome allowed her to ease out of his embrace far enough to take a deep breath, she looked into his happy, smiling face and grinned back at him.

''I guess you realize you got your wish,'' she said, a tremor of emotion still evident in her voice. ''I love you. I love you so much. You know that, don't you?''

''I'm beginning to.'' His smile got broader. ''You are going to marry me, aren't you?''

''You bet I am,'' Abby said, joy bubbling in her laugh and shining out of her eyes.

''And darn soon, I hope.''

"How soon would you like?"

"I'd like tomorrow, but I suppose arranging a wedding takes more time than that, doesn't it?"

"Yes, it certainly does," Abby replied as staunchly as she could manage with Rome's sensual gaze appraising her, and his thumb caressing her lower lip. "How would you feel about Christmastime?"

"Perfect! Christmas it is," he declared buoyantly. "That will also give you time to pick out just the perfect place you'd like me to take you for our honeymoon."

"Oh, I know the one and only place for our honeymoon right now." Her tone was confident, and she offered him a knowing smile.

"Okay, where is it?"

"Well, Rome, where else would a bona fide member of the clan of Douglas take his bride but Scotland!"

Rome's hearty laugh was jubilant. "Abby, you beautiful, darling you, I couldn't agree with you more." He took her in his arms again, and as she melted closer to him and felt the loving drumbeats of his heart, joy spread over her and around her, wrapping her in the warm, fulfilling elation of loving and being loved.

DATE DUE

APR 10 '98			
APR 28 '98			
MAY 21 '98			
JUN 23 '98			
AUG 1 7 '98			
DEC 0 7 '98			
DEC 2 1 '98			
JAN 1 8 '00			
MAR 0 3 '00			

Charlotte County Library
P.O. Box 788
Charlotte C.H., VA 23923

DEMCO

Chapter One

The painted sign hanging from the crossbar on the lantern post swung gently back and forth in the summer breeze. It was not a large sign, and the simple block letters spelled out HAMPTON HOUSE ANTIQUES. Abby Hampton stood at one of the front windows of the late-eighteenth-century house watching as a tall, athletic-looking man unfolded himself out of a bullet-shaped sports car. He was like one of those fold-up measuring tools carpenters use, for his lean, angular body emerged from the car twelve inches at a time, and when he straightened to his full height he appeared to be well over six feet tall.

The man was punctual, that was one thing she now knew about Rome Douglas. He'd telephoned her earlier this morning asking for an appointment at eleven o'clock. His name was not one she'd heard before, and nothing in his speech held a familiar New England sound. She hoped he was an informed, antique-seeking tourist who'd heard that Lindenwood, New Hampshire, was a haven for antiques, as well as being a truly picturesque town in the White Mountains. If he were, that would prove interesting, but somehow she

1

feared he was more apt to be an out-of-state dealer hoping to talk her out of some prized antiques at a vast discount. That would explain why he'd called for an appointment. The usual antique shopper liked to brouse leisurely and did not call ahead. Although some of Abby's regular out-of-town customers did occasionally check with her before they made a trip over to Lindenwood, especially if they thought she'd been away on a buying trip and would have a group of new things for them to see.

Abby ceased speculating, knowing her curiosity would soon be put to rest. The cherry wood tall clock in the entry hall now indicated the hour by striking eleven times, and then the doorbell chimed its two musical notes announcing the very punctual arrival of Mr. Rome Douglas.

"Come in—the door's open," Abby called out as she walked from the living room toward the front door. She arrived in the entry hall just as Rome had stepped inside and was closing the door behind him.

"Hi, you must be Abigail Hampton." His boldly handsome face smiled warmly down at her.

Abby considered herself tall, for she was five foot seven. But now, standing next to this auburn-haired stranger, she felt almost petite. "How did you know my name?" she asked, her violet-blue eyes narrowing curiously.

"Well you see, I needed to find out the owner of

the historic Hampton House, which, as of course you know, is the earliest house built in Lindenwood. I checked the records at the courthouse and there was your name, Abigail Leeds Hampton.''

"I might have guessed you learned that from some dusty old files," she said, wrinkling her nose in a grimace. "No one but my grandmother for whom I was named ever called me Abigail. I'm Abby," she said, with an emphatic bob of her head.

"Abby—I like that much better. Sounds friendly and nice. I think an Abby will prove more agreeable to do business with than an Abigail." There was a touch of humor now around his generous mouth and near his moss-green eyes, which gleamed with shadows of deep gold.

Amused by this rather foolish discussion of her name, Abby laughed and said, "I want you to know that I'm agreeable to selling you antiques no matter what you call me. Just tell me what sort of things you're interested in—period furniture possibly, or some area of collectibles?''

"Oh, I'm afraid I've misled you." His expression sobered, and the levity was gone from his voice. "I'm here to do business with you all right, but it's not to buy antiques.''

"Really, then what is it about?" she asked, her dark eyebrows slanting in a frown.

"You see, I'm with Allied Studios, Abby. I'm here

scouting a location for a film," he explained with a bland smile. "Could we, perhaps, sit down someplace and discuss the project?"

Abby shrugged. "Yes, I suppose we can. But I can't imagine why on earth you should want to talk to me about the filming of some movie."

"Because this is a major production that requires an authentic New England setting down to the last detail. I'm confident that you can provide part of what I'm looking for."

Abby doubted that, but his air of self-assurance aroused her curiosity. Besides, she had nothing to lose by hearing him out. "Come on then. We'll have to go to the back of the house. I use the front rooms to display the antiques I sell," she said, turning and leading him toward a door at the far end of the entry hall. She walked with an easy grace, her lustrous dark hair barely touching her proud shoulders.

Abby led Rome Douglas to the rear parlor of the Federal-style house that dated back to 1796. This second parlor, located off the kitchen, was an attractive room with a small fireplace, a slant-front desk, and a mahogany tea table with a pair of armchairs and two matching side chairs.

"I have coffee made, if you'd like a cup," Abby offered graciously.

"No thanks," Rome answered with a negative shake of his head. "I've just come from a meeting with the mayor and several members of your chamber of commerce, and I drank coffee with them. But don't let me stop you from having a cup,'' he said amiably.

''I had some earlier too. So let's just sit down and you can tell me all about what you're planning to do here in our little town.'' She took a seat in one of the armchairs, motioning to Rome to do the same.

''Did you happen to read a popular novel that came out a couple of years ago entitled *A Different Drummer*?'' he asked her, as he settled into the chair across the table from her.

''Yeah, I did—all five or six hundred pages of it. I like those multigeneration family sagas. All that laughing and crying, living and dying, loving and hating, you get the whole nine yards in that book. We sentimental women love that, you know.'' There was a glint of humor in her eyes as she added this.

''Allied Studios is counting on that very fact.'' He measured her with an appraising look. ''And I'm counting on the fact that since you liked the book so much you're going to want to see it made into a great movie.''

Abby inclined her head, interest quickening on her face. ''Then that's the film you plan to shoot here?''

He nodded. ''Don't you agree that Lindenwood could easily double for Kerryville, the town in *A Different Drummer*?''

Abby thought about this for a minute before she answered. ''I suppose it does come pretty close at that. But then there are lots of towns like Lindenwood in

New Hampshire, as well as all through Vermont and Connecticut. Don't get me wrong, it would prove exciting for quiet little Lindenwood to be the location for your movie. Sure would stir things up around here. But I'm curious to know why you'd choose it? What's our special appeal?''

''Well for starters, Lindenwood has the ideal setup we require. You have a picturesque public square with a courthouse, town hall, post office, two national banks, a public library, and an assortment of commercial shops. Change the signs on a few storefronts and—presto!'' Rome made a sweeping gesture with his hands. ''You have a replica of Kerryville.''

''If you say so,'' she said, laughing at his histrionics.

''And that's not all Lindenwood has to offer. There's your park and that nice lake with the Indian name that I never can remember, and the white steepled church next to a two-hundred-year-old cemetery. Our cameramen will be rapturous when they view all that. In fact, all the outdoor scenes can be shot with a minimum of additions.''

''You make it sound like all you have to do is bring in the actors and the camera crews and start rolling,'' she said, studying him with a musing look.

''No, we're not that far yet.'' He wagged his head in a negative fashion. ''There's something vitally important that I still have to acquire.'' He leaned toward her. ''That's what I came to see you about. I want to